Raquel had not
the least with

She hadn't expected their swim to be cut short, but neither of them could very well turn their backs on the sexual attraction that had been brewing, as much as she had tried to deny it. They continued to kiss as though they'd been doing so for years. Her breasts heaved and Raquel felt her nipples tingling like crazy. She could not remember a time when a man's kiss had aroused her so.

And clearly Keanu was experiencing a similar carnal reaction. With her leg wound around his below the pulsating water, she could feel his erection just begging to be let out of his swim briefs. Only this wasn't the time or place for that. Was it? And should they be moving in that direction so quickly?

They were practically making love in the spa right now, which was a bit too brazen for Raquel, no matter how good it felt. She pried their mouths apart.

"Maybe this isn't such a good idea," Raquel said.

He touched her wet hair. "Or maybe it's a great idea?"

"We should slow down," she said.

"Why should we?" Keanu said. "Don't we deserve to play this out and let our feelings guide us?"

Raquel's body screamed yes, but her mind was still leery about going down that path. After all, they were still doing business together. But this was *anything* but business.

Books by Devon Vaughn Archer

Kimani Romance

Christmas Heat
Destined to Meet
Kissing the Man Next Door
Christmas Diamonds
Pleasure in Hawaii
Private Luau

Kimani Arabesque

Love Once Again

DEVON VAUGHN ARCHER

is the bestselling author of more than a dozen mainstream and romance novels. He was the first male author to write a solo novel for Harlequin's Arabesque line with *Love Once Again*. His other recent novels include *The Hitman's Woman*, holiday romances *Christmas Diamonds* and *Christmas Heat*, *Kissing the Man Next Door*, *Destined To Meet* and the bestselling young-adult coming-of-age ebook, *Her Teen Dream*. Most of the author's books can be found in Kindle and Nook versions. Devon resides in the Pacific Northwest with his wife, where he is busy working on his next novel. Keep up with the author and his writings on Twitter, Facebook, LinkedIn, MySpace, Goodreads, LibraryThing and Book Town, and www.devonvaughnarcher.com.

PRIVATE
Luau

Devon Vaughn Archer

KIMANI
ROMANCE

To my wonderful mother, Marjah Aljean,
who still dreams of going to Hawaii,
and will be able to through the magic of this novel.

And to all my wonderful fans who love romance fiction
and the romantic spirit that lives in Hawaii.

KIMANI PRESS™

Recycling programs
for this product may
not exist in your area.

ISBN-13: 978-0-373-86239-9

PRIVATE LUAU

Copyright © 2011 by R. Barri Flowers

www.kimanipress.com

Printed in U.S.A.

Dear Reader,

I am so thrilled that you have chosen *Private Luau* to read. I consider it to be a wonderful tropical island romance and travelogue in one.

It takes place in breathtaking Honolulu on the wondrous island of Oahu, where my heroine, an image consultant, takes on the task of reshaping the image of a former NBA bad boy, now a hunk who's got his eye on her professionally and romantically.

Private Luau is the second title in my Passions in Paradise series, with each story taking place on a different Hawaiian island. The inspiration for this series comes from my own frequent travels to Hawaii with my wife, giving us the opportunity to renew our love time and time again in paradise.

You are sure to fall in love with Honolulu and the characters as you turn the pages.

The third book in the series will be out in 2012.

Best,

Devon

I would like to thank my gorgeous wife, nicknamed Maui Mermaid, for her loving support over the years and inspiration in putting forth my best efforts to find success as a writer while staying grounded.

Thanks also goes to the Harlequin and Kimani staff for their roles in bringing this novel to fruition and making it available to readers around the world.

Chapter 1

Raquel Deneuve sat at her desk on the third floor of the Mele office building in downtown Honolulu, wondering where the year had gone. It seemed like only yesterday she was ringing in the New Year with her mother and friends. Now it was only four months till January first rolled around again. She would love to toast champagne with a love interest this time. What could be better than that to start a new year, and in beautiful Hawaii to boot? The problem was that time was running out, and there were no real prospects on the horizon. Certainly not her last boyfriend, who she had dumped six months ago, because of his lack of initiative and decidedly weak work ethic. She hadn't built up her career as a professional coach and personal consultant only to support someone who was going nowhere fast.

Oh well, live and learn. If there was someone else out there waiting to steal her heart, she was available and willing to meet him halfway. If not, she wouldn't cry about it. At thirty-three, there was still plenty of time to wait for true love to blossom, even if her mother begged to differ and believed that her biological clock demanded that she think in terms of sooner than later. As far as Raquel was concerned, the here and now was just fine, even without a man in her life. Aside from an occupation that was keeping her very busy, she had a part-time gig as a hula dancer. She considered it a great way to unwind, have fun and stay in shape.

Raquel's reverie was interrupted by the phone ringing. She lifted the handset and saw from the caller ID that it was her assistant.

"There's a Richard Brock on the line," she said. "Do you want me to put him through?"

Raquel recognized the name, having done business before with the mega agent of athletes, albeit not recently. "Yes, please," she responded.

"Will do."

Raquel took a breath and readied herself to speak to the man she had been slightly intimidated by, given that he was old enough to be her father and was worth a mint, thanks to those he had gotten lucrative contracts for.

"Aloha to you over there in Honolulu," Richard said in a gravelly voice.

"Aloha, Richard." She was pretty sure he was still based in New York City. "It's been too long."

"Yes, it has."

Raquel recalled when he'd come to Hawaii a couple of years ago and hired her as a corporate image expert to speak at a seminar he was giving. By his account and others, she'd earned high marks.

"How can I help you?" she asked professionally.

"Being a longtime Hawaii resident and sports fan, if memory serves me correctly, I'm sure you're familiar with basketball star Keanu Bailey, aren't you?"

Raquel smiled. Local boy makes good. First at a local college and then in the NBA as an all-star guard for a couple of teams. Who in Honolulu hadn't heard of him? Even though not everything she'd heard had cast the man in a favorable light.

"Yes, I'm well aware of Mr. Bailey," she said, though their paths had never crossed. "He retired recently, didn't he?"

"At the end of last season," Richard told her. "Personally, I thought he could still play at a high level for a couple more years, but that's just me. Anyway, Keanu is one of my clients and he's just moved back to Honolulu where he kept a summer home."

"Good for him." Raquel ran a hand through her wavy, long hair with envy. She'd seen Keanu's "summer" home on a TV news program and could only imagine what his year-round place must have looked like.

"You probably know that throughout his career, Keanu has been portrayed as a bad boy, hard partier and womanizer, among other things," Richard said.

And deservedly so, it would seem. She recalled some of his antics and temper tantrums on the court, leading to a fair share of technicals and automatic suspensions. Keanu's penchant for partying hard and often was practically legendary. As for the womanizing, it seemed as if every up-and-coming gorgeous actress, singer and model had been photographed on his arm at one time or another.

"Yes, I'm aware," Raquel acknowledged.

"Well, real or not, Keanu would like to try and change that image now that he's retired," Richard said. "I've advised him that now that he's away from the game and older, he needs a makeover to maintain his marketability. He agreed." Richard paused. "Do you think you can help him?"

Raquel was admittedly piqued by the notion, though she needed to talk to Keanu first to see if he was really serious about revamping his image. Otherwise people would see right through it, and he might be even worse off.

"I'd love to try," she said. She thought of the possibility of future referrals from Richard and suddenly gained a burst of confidence. "Yes, I can definitely help Mr. Bailey improve his image!"

"Wonderful. Here's Keanu's private number. I'll give him a heads-up that you'll be calling and you two can work out the details."

"Sounds good." Raquel had barely hung up when her girlfriend, Lauren Newberg, called.

"Hey, I just wanted to make sure we were still on for girls' night out," Lauren said, as the sounds of her television echoed in the background.

"Absolutely," Raquel told her. Since they had planned this more than a week ago, she saw no reason to back out now. Besides, it would give her time to speak with Keanu before sharing the news that she would be working with one of Lauren's favorite basketball players. Though Raquel admired the undeniable talents that he'd shown on the court, admittedly her favorite basketball players these days were LeBron James and Derrick Rose.

"Great," Lauren said. "I'll meet you there at eight—and don't be late."

Raquel smiled. "I won't be. Look, I hate to cut this short, but I've got to call a potential client."

"Don't let me stop you," Lauren said. "I'm on my way out the door to see if I can drum up some business." She was an account executive for an internet-based company. "Later."

Raquel disconnected and went to her computer. She used Google to search Keanu Bailey to see what other tidbits she could learn about the man before calling him to arrange a meeting.

Keanu Bailey drove his black Mercedes down Diamond Head Road, admiring the ocean even while his mind was absorbed with wondering what life had in store for him now that he'd officially retired from the NBA. He'd had a nice run of fourteen years, more than the average player, and made the most of it—spending the first half with the Los Angeles Lakers before moving on to the Detroit Pistons and finishing his career there. It had been gut-wrenching to walk away from the only thing he'd ever done as work, if you could call it that. But even though he still had a deadly jumper and could occasionally put on enough speed to get by someone and go to the hole, Keanu knew it was time to hang it up. The younger guards were often taller than his six-four and quicker than he'd ever been, making it a chore to try and keep up with them. He decided it was best to go out on his own terms, while he was still considered by many to be near the top of his game and a perennial all-star.

Now he was back in his hometown of Honolulu where he was an All-American in high school and a starting point guard for the University of Hawaii before being drafted in the first round by the Lakers. Keanu drove onto 22nd Avenue while wondering what the hell he would do with his life now. He'd invested his money wisely over the years and would never have to worry about earning a living, but that didn't mean he was content to just sit back and do nothing. He wanted to make a meaningful contribution to society and also keep his brand alive.

According to his agent, Richard Brock, the Keanu Bailey brand had taken a hit in recent years because of a bad rap for his on-the-court competitiveness and his off-the-court romances—which had admittedly been many, though none had gone very far at the end of the day. He hated being compared to Rasheed Wallace and Tiger Woods, feeling that he wasn't nearly as hot-tempered as Rasheed or the reckless ladies' man Tiger turned out to be. Not to mention those who felt he was more self-centered than most, even if Keanu begged to differ. Try telling that to the media that made money by misleading images and exaggerated words. From what Richard told him, it was up to Keanu to improve his image for the better.

So Richard had hooked him up with a local image consultant. Keanu wasn't entirely convinced that was the answer, but since Richard had always done right by him and was still representing him, he decided to follow his advice and give this woman a try.

Keanu had reached the barbershop when his iPhone

rang. He saw that it was the call he'd been waiting for and climbed out of the car, allowing the noontime sun to beat down on his chiseled, caramel-complexioned face before answering it.

"Hi, this is Raquel Deneuve from Deneuve Corporate and Personal Communications."

He liked the soft, even pitch of her voice and wondered if she matched up in appearance. "Good to hear from you, Ms. Deneuve," he said coolly. "Richard told me he had spoken with you."

"Yes. So I understand you're in need of an image makeover."

He chuckled. "You could say that. I think it would be a good thing for me as I start the next phase of my life."

"I'd be happy to help you achieve your goals in that regard," Raquel said. "I'm available this afternoon at three to talk face-to-face if that works for you."

"Yeah, that'll work." Somehow Keanu couldn't imagine that she wasn't fine. He'd soon find out by checking her out online.

"I'm in the Mele office building downtown on Bethel Street. It's next to the Fort Street Mall."

"I'll see you at three," Keanu told her and disconnected. He was curious as to how she might improve his image without sacrificing his core principles. Whatever it took to make this succeed, he was willing to do his part. He headed inside the barbershop, ready to get his new image started with a haircut.

Raquel was eager to meet her new client, though in a way she felt as if she had known him for years. Or at least she knew his professional and public faces, along with his reputation. She would give him the benefit of the doubt that he was serious about this and that it wasn't just a publicity stunt on his part designed to get a little sympathy from an overzealous media before drifting back into his old ways.

She had learned from the internet that Keanu had averaged twenty-two points a game last season with the Pistons to lead the team in scoring. But his assists had gone down while his technicals had gone up. Apparently he was dating or had been recently involved with Cassandra Tucker, an award-winning actress currently starring in the hit TV crime series *Dark Intentions*. Somehow Raquel couldn't imagine being romantically involved with an athlete. How would she ever be able to trust him—especially when he had a bad track record—or compete with the groupies for his affection?

"Your three o'clock appointment is here," Raquel's assistant told her over the phone.

"Send him in."

Raquel felt just a touch of butterflies in her stomach. She was used to high-profile clients. But rarely had she encountered one who had almost become larger than life. Maybe that was part of Keanu Bailey's image problem. He needed to come back down to earth and be normal again. Or might that be asking too much from someone who was surely full of himself and had others giving him a free pass in life?

She glanced quickly at a mirror she kept in the drawer. It wouldn't do to have her makeup smeared. First impressions worked both ways. Everything looked just fine, including her hair, which had been styled just yesterday. She stood from her high-backed leather desk chair and smoothed the back of her pleated skirt and straightened her suit jacket. Matching slingback wedges added a couple of inches to her five-eight height, which she knew would still put her several inches below Keanu's height.

Raquel was halfway to the door when Keanu walked in, wearing a slightly crooked smile on a sexy wide mouth. Her first thought was that he was even better looking in person. *How about extremely handsome?* His black hair was cut in a skin fade hairstyle, bordering the brown sugar skin tone of his square-jawed face. There was a cleft in his chin, deepened with the grin. A white gold diamond earring was in his left earlobe. She glanced at the muscled contours of his body, covered in a Detroit Pistons gray jersey, along with the striped black athletic pants, and his own brand of sneakers.

Raquel watched her arm shoot straight toward him like a robot as she said, "Mr. Bailey, it's nice to meet you."

"You too, Ms. Deneuve," Keanu offered in a deep voice and covered her hand with his as they shook.

He stared down at her with probably the most compelling gray-sable eyes she had ever seen, causing Raquel to flinch as she took back her hand.

"Please call me Raquel," she told him.

"Only if you'll call me Keanu," he said suavely. "I'll leave the Mr. Bailey bit to my Uncle Sonny."

Raquel recalled reading about him being raised by his uncle, who was a celebrated local high school basketball coach and school athletic director before retiring a few years ago. She flashed a smile at him. "All right, Keanu. Please sit down."

She inclined her head toward the two chairs in front of her desk and waited for him to choose one before she moved toward the other. Raquel could see that he'd been checking her out just as she had assessed him. She wondered if he was comparing her to all the beautiful women he had no doubt bedded. Or had she captivated him all on her own?

Not that it mattered. They were there for business. Anything else would simply get in the way of their mutual goals.

"So you're looking to improve your image, huh?" she said in a friendly tone to get them started.

That crooked grin played on his lips again. "Yeah, it could use a little adjustment now that I'm retired from basketball."

Raquel peered at him. "And exactly what would you like to see adjusted?" She needed to know how he perceived himself before they could move forward.

"Well, I'd like to be taken seriously as an even-tempered, charitable, down-to-earth, one-woman man who isn't just looking for the next party to attend, but is available for speaking engagements and the right product endorsements."

"That's an ambitious agenda," Raquel said, impressed that he had obviously given it some forethought and was genuinely looking to discard the bad reputation.

"I always shoot for the stars," Keanu practically bragged, sitting back comfortably.

"You certainly did that in the NBA," she cracked, thinking of his rainbow jumpers. "When you were in the 'zone,' there was no stopping you."

He laughed. "Yeah, I suppose I could bring it home from time to time when it was called for."

Raquel found herself taken with the richness of his

laughter and imagined she could listen to it all day long. And stare into those wondrous eyes or at his incredibly sexy mouth. Then there was the dimple on his chin, which she'd always found sexy on men. She quickly pulled back from such intimate thoughts, as this wasn't the time or place.

She cleared her throat. "Well, it will certainly take some work to reform your image," she said. "Based on the little research I've done, you definitely seem to have a major PR problem."

"Ouch." Keanu held his stomach as if he had been hit by a boxer.

Raquel almost felt his pain. "Just being honest. I'm sure you expect no less from me in working with you."

"True." He met her eyes squarely. "Go ahead and let me have it. I just want to get this going."

"All right." She took a breath, understanding that big egos are part of what makes an athlete successful. Unfortunately, it also made it more difficult to come to terms with faults, though Keanu had taken a big step in the right direction by attempting to improve his image. "Well, to start with, your temper tantrums on court are well-known. That needs to be rechanneled in more constructive ways that we can work on."

Keanu's mouth tightened. "I've always been a competitor. The fact that it was sometimes misconstrued, especially during the early part of my career, doesn't make the rap the real deal."

"So all those technical fouls you received were simply misinterpreted as pushing people around or the fault of the referees and other players?" She hoped she didn't sound too sarcastic.

Keanu chuckled. "I take my share of the blame for

any heated exchanges as part of the game," he said tersely. "But I also know for a fact that for me it was *always* about winning fair and square. Or giving one hundred percent every time I was out there. If that meant getting in someone's face from time to time, so be it."

Raquel took mental notes, but had no quarrel with his philosophy, per se. Especially since it related only to winning. She might have a different opinion if it pertained to life in the real world.

"So I see that you've endorsed or created a number of products over the years, including your own cologne and shoe brand." She looked down at his unmarred black sneakers and wondered if he put on a new pair every day. "Unfortunately, those are all about you. I see less of an effort to give back to the community."

"Hey, I do signings for kids every now and then," Keanu said defensively. "I've also donated to charity over the years."

"That's true of most athletes." She paused, acknowledging that much. "You may need to go further in showing there is much more to you than the generosity of your time."

"Whatever you think. I'm open to suggestions."

Raquel liked that he seemed to be flexible, which wasn't always the case with her clients. "You'll definitely have to tone down on the party life," she told him. "It may have its place when one wants to let loose, but not if you want to present a more mature, less merrymaking image."

Keanu stiffened. "I hear you. I'm definitely up for getting past that stage, though I see no reason why

having fun with friends needs to interfere with showing I can also be a serious individual."

"I'm not saying you have to become a monk. Just a
need to lighten up on that aspect of what you bring to
the table."

"Hey, I've probably partied only half as much as
many other athletes I know."

"Good for you, but they're not my clients," Raquel
said bluntly, not wanting to pat him on the back for jus-
tifying behavior that had apparently gotten out of control at times. "Though I suspect some of them may also
find themselves in need of image makeovers as they get
older and want to reinvent themselves."

"I wouldn't be surprised," Keanu allowed, scratch-
ing his chin thoughtfully. "As for me, it's not so much
about reinventing myself, per se. 'Cause I'm cool with
who I am inside. It's more about getting the real person
out front and center."

Well said and you may even believe it. But, in her
experience, the public facade more often than not re-
flected one's true essence as much as any part that may
have been hiding within. She doubted it was any different in this case, though she always refrained from judging a client prematurely. Even one whose life and times
had been chronicled on television and in the media for
years.

Raquel gazed at Keanu, anticipating his reaction to
her next observation. "Whether real or exaggerated,
perhaps the area you need to work on most is your reputation for being a womanizer." He'd mentioned earlier
about wanting to be a one-woman man. Was he serious? Or was that merely for her benefit? "Seems like

you've bedded half the women in Hollywood and the recording industry, if the tabloids are to be believed."

Keanu flashed his teeth. They were sparkling white and, as far as Raquel could determine, showed no sign of the damage he'd once sustained after being accidentally elbowed by a teammate while fighting for a rebound. He lost the smile abruptly and narrowed his gaze.

"Don't believe everything you read," he admonished her. "Especially considering the sources that put that stuff out."

Raquel's curly lashes fluttered skeptically. "Are you saying you're not a *player* off the court?" She told herself the question was strictly professional, even if he was the type of man she was physically attracted to under the right circumstances.

"Look, I'm not going to lie to you. I've had my fair share of flings with beautiful ladies, in getting caught up in all the temptations that come with the territory as an NBA player. But I'm trying to get away from all that today."

"Oh, really?" At least he admitted that the gossip was not entirely unfounded.

"Yeah. I'm just looking to chill, enjoy life after pro basketball, settle down with one special lady, and have people see the real Keanu Bailey." He gave her a straight look. "And that's where you come in."

Raquel got a warm feeling knowing that he was putting his trust in her to help transform his image. She looked forward to the assignment. She wasn't sure she bought into the settle down with one special lady bit, as it seemed to her that it would be hard, if not impossible to give up all the eye candy and hot bodies that were likely to present themselves to him for some time to come. But if she could help him clean up his act even a little in this regard, it could do wonders for his marketability. She gave him her hourly fees, wanting everything to be up front, though she suspected money was no object for him. From what she gathered, he'd made millions in the NBA and investments and hadn't blown it all like some of his contemporaries.

Keanu accepted her terms without blinking an eye. "Now that we're working together, this may seem out of left field, but would you like to go out to dinner with me?"

"Excuse me?" she asked, though Raquel had heard him perfectly.

"I thought maybe we could grab a bite somewhere, get to know each other better." His voice lowered an octave. "Or at least give me the chance to get to know you a bit more."

She cocked an eyebrow. "Are you actually asking me out on a date?"

His cleft widened with a slow, sexy grin. "Would that be so wrong if I were? You're a very beautiful woman, I'm sure I don't have to tell you. I just think—"

"Hold it right there." Raquel checked him, lifting her hand to that effect. "I appreciate the compliment and offer to go out. Unfortunately, I don't mix business with pleasure." Not only that, but she wasn't going to be another woman he bedded before moving on to someone else. Was this simply more playing the field when he was supposed to be backing away from that lifestyle? If so, this could prove to be a bigger project than she had bargained for.

* * *

"I understand," Keanu told Raquel, hiding his disappointment. "You can't blame a man for trying."

"I think we'd better just stay focused on repairing your image and not adding to it adversely," she said flatly.

He smiled thinly. "Whatever you say."

Keanu was admittedly transfixed with his new image consultant's ravishing beauty. It went way beyond what he had imagined when talking to her over the phone. Raquel Deneuve made even the best-looking women he'd known seem average with her honey complexion, luscious long brown hair with plenty of waves and curls, big, bold café au lait eyes, ample ruby lips and an hourglass figure that spoke to him even within that sharp suit she wore. From the moment he'd laid eyes on her, virtually all Keanu could think about was wanting to take her to bed. He had no doubt that their naked bodies would fit together perfectly.

But he understood that asking her out so soon went against the grain and he could respect that. It gave the impression that he was every bit what the tabloids had made him out to be: a man interested in bedding every nice-looking woman to cross his path. That wasn't the case at all. Not this time. There was something about Raquel that captured his fancy—and not just her looks. He liked her style, intelligence, poise, sexiness and even her professionalism, having taken it all in with just one initial meeting.

He would play it her way for now and give their business arrangement a chance to work. Beyond that, Keanu liked the thought of having someone like Raquel in his personal life and bed, and was tired of the come-and-go women of the past. She was the kind of lady with whom he wouldn't mind one bit having a steady relationship. Judging by the way the sparks between them were flying left and right, he'd have to say the feeling was very much mutual. Or was that only his imagination?

Keanu got to his feet and waited for Raquel to do the same. "When would you like to get together again, professionally speaking?"

"I'll give you my card," she said, grabbing one off her desk and handing it to him. "It has my office and cell phone numbers."

"Thanks." He stuck the card in his pocket, but kept his eyes solidly on her.

She smiled faintly. "Of course, I have your contact information as well. We'll figure out a good time for both of us to meet again."

"Fair enough." He studied her remarkable lips, wishing he could kiss them right there on the spot, their fullness so enticing. Keanu forced his eyes to shift to hers and stuck out his hand. "I appreciate your taking me on," he spoke sincerely.

Raquel shook his hand. "I'm happy to do so. Besides, Richard Brock sees you as anything but a lost cause. I'm sure neither of us wants to let him down."

"Of course not." Keanu loved the softness of her skin and the movement of Raquel's long, thin fingers against his palm. The thought of those fingers caressing his body aroused him. Did she sense that? Or was it better that she didn't at this point?

Chapter 2

When Raquel left the office an hour later, she still hadn't quite been able to shake the impression Keanu Bailey had left on her, his bad boy reputation notwithstanding. The man had definite sex appeal and she could well imagine how easily women had fallen under his spell, especially with those enchanting gray-brown eyes boring into her. Not to mention the women who were caught up in the glamorous lifestyle of rich and famous athletes. She certainly did not fall into that category. She didn't need a man's stature or wealth, having done just fine in those categories on her own.

While she was certainly in the market for boyfriend material, and Keanu had everything she could want in a man physically, Raquel was not about to go down that road with her celebrity client. Not even if he was obviously into her and flattered her with his compliment about her looks. If they were to succeed in business, getting together on a personal level was not a good idea for either of them.

Was it?

Raquel drove her Subaru Legacy down Pensacola Street en route to Makiki Heights, where her mother lived. Having grown up in the neighborhood as a military brat, she found the familiarity of the mostly older homes, apartment buildings and maze of side streets comforting. As an only child, her parents had spoiled her rotten and she loved them for it. Her father died a few years ago, leaving only Raquel's mother to check on. She had recently begun dating again and Raquel was all for it, knowing her father would not have wanted her mother to spend the rest of her life alone.

He wouldn't want that for me either, Raquel told herself as she turned onto Haiki Place. But he also wouldn't want her to settle for less. Until she found the right man at the right time, she would be patient and focus on other things, such as building her client list. Keanu Bailey was certainly a nice one to add to her growing portfolio.

She pulled into the driveway of her mother's single-story house. It offered a great view of the city and wasn't too far from Raquel's condominium in Waikiki. Stepping onto the lanai, she rang the bell, choosing not to use her key to respect her mother's privacy. Not that there was any indication she had company. But better safe than sorry.

Davetta Deneuve opened the door. "Did you lose your key?"

Raquel smiled and eyed her fifty-nine-year-old mother, who could have easily passed for ten years younger. She was slender and nearly as tall as Raquel with a reddish-brown stacked bob. "No, I just didn't want to barge in on you," she explained, walking onto the hickory wooden floor inside the living room.

"Since when?" Davetta fluttered her lashes, closing the door.

Raquel glanced around at the contemporary furnishings. "Since you began hooking up with…what's his name again?"

"Sean. And don't worry about him. We're taking it nice and slow."

"Weren't you the one who told me that putting on some speed was the only way to go?" Raquel teased her, while happy to see that her mother was not jumping into something too soon.

Davetta smiled. "Yes, for my daughter who can't or won't settle down with a nice young man, have babies and…"

"I know, a white picket fence," Raquel finished what had become a routine speech in recent times. "It doesn't always work that way in real life." Certainly not in her life as yet.

"Just know that you don't have forever, even if it sometimes seems that way," Davetta warned. "Your job can *only* take you so far in being happy."

"It'll just have to suffice for now. And I'm perfectly content with that."

"Do you want something to eat?" Davetta asked.

"I can't stay," Raquel told her. "I just wanted to drop by on the way home and see how you were doing."

"As you can see, I'm fine."

"Good." Raquel gave her a hug. "I'll see you later. Be sure to tell Sean I said hello."

"I will." Davetta walked with her toward the door. "And if you want to double date sometime with your mother, just let me know. I'm sure it would be interesting."

"No doubt." Raquel smiled at the thought while remaining noncommittal. Would most men find that appealing or run-for-the-hills scary? How would Keanu feel about going out on a date with her mother looking over his shoulder? Should she even be imagining such a thing with her newest and most intriguing client?

Raquel lived in Waikiki Place, an upscale high-rise, located on Kalakaua Avenue and just minutes from downtown Honolulu and her place of work, as well as some great places to dine and shop. She had decided to invest in the affordable two-bedroom residence that was within walking distance to the beach two years ago and loved it. The mountain, water and sunset views were amazing from her lanai. She had given the place and its feng shui architecture her special touch, blending Queen Anne furniture with classic modern furnishings. It was a perfect match to go with the plum carpeting and beige walls that she had textured with stucco. Raquel considered the state-of-the-art fitness center in Waikiki Place to be one of the most attractive features, as she loved to work out so her body could handle the rigors of hula dancing.

She stepped inside the gourmet kitchen and warmed some leftovers for dinner. Though a pretty good cook, lately Raquel had found little time or desire to cook anything elaborate for herself. She imagined that Keanu Bailey had a big appetite for some delicious soul food, even if it seemed there wasn't an ounce of fat on his frame. If their professional relationship worked out well, maybe she would invite him over some day for a tasty meal.

After freshening up, Raquel changed into a black-and-magenta sleeveless ruched dress and open-toe pumps for ladies' night out with Lauren. She couldn't wait to tell her that Keanu was now a client and would probably be happy to give her his autograph. Raquel didn't believe Keanu was Lauren's type as far as dating material. She wasn't sure exactly what type of woman Keanu preferred, as he seemed to have been involved with every type imaginable at one time or another. Or was she getting carried away by exaggerations of the press, which he had suggested was the case?

Keanu drove past the gate and onto his property in the prestigious Kahala neighborhood of Honolulu. Located between the Waialae Country Club and Diamond Head crater, he had purchased the secluded beach-front mansion five years ago for four million dollars as a summer home and investment property. His Uncle Sonny and his wife Ashley lived there, occupying one wing of the 7,000-square-foot, eight-bedroom, two-story estate. Now that he had decided to make Hono-lulu his retirement home, Keanu had moved into the other wing, allowing him plenty of privacy without in-truding on his uncle's space.

He stepped inside the double French entry doors, still thinking about Raquel Deneuve, his lovely new image consultant. With a shapely body like hers, he imagined she could have been a model, actress, or anything she chose to be. Lucky for him that Raquel was right where she was and that Richard had hooked him up with her.

Keanu felt that if he played his cards right, he just might get to see what lay beyond her professionalism.

Keanu found the man who raised him in the enormous kitchen, making dinner. It was something that had become a habit ever since he'd retired as a high school basketball coach three years ago. After losing his parents as a child and being taken in by his uncle, Keanu considered him to be more than just a father figure. He credited Sonny Bailey with honing his basketball skills early on in life, giving him the opportunity to become a star in high school and make it to the NBA.

"Hey, Unc," Keanu said. Sonny had been deeply engrossed in seasoning some pork chops.

Sonny turned around and broke into a smile. "Hey there."

"Smells good." Keanu smiled at the man who was his height and thicker in the midsection with closely cropped gray hair.

"It's going to taste even better. I hope you've brought your appetite back with you."

Keanu grinned. "Oh yeah, it's still there."

"Good. That's what I like to hear."

"Can I help with anything?" Keanu offered.

"Got it covered." Sonny looked at him. "I like your haircut."

"It needed to be done," Keanu said, running a hand across the top of his head.

"For you, or is there some new woman in your life I don't know about?"

Keanu chuckled. He only wished that were the case. He had pretty much been on a break from women and all their drama, thinking it was better to be on his own for a while. Then he met Raquel, who stirred the blood inside him, making Keanu wonder if he had met someone truly worth pursuing.

"Actually there is a new woman in my life," he said, grabbing a celery stick.

"Oh yeah?" Sonny flashed his teeth. "I thought so."

"Not what you think." Not yet anyway.

"Care to enlighten me?" his uncle asked.

"I've hired an image consultant," Keanu told him.

Sonny cocked a bushy brow. "I think your image is fine. So what if a few jerks in the media have given you a hard time."

"My agent thinks it's a good idea to try and reform that a bit," Keanu explained. "I think it's worth a shot."

"If you say so," Sonny told him. "I'll support you, whatever you want to do."

"Thanks." Keanu felt his stomach growl. "Once I see what Raquel has in mind, I'll have a better idea of what she thinks I need to do."

"Just don't change the person you really are at the core," Sonny said. "No matter what others may think they see or know of you."

"I'll always be me," Keanu promised, happy to know that was good enough for his uncle.

"Hello, Keanu," he heard a voice say. Turning around, Keanu saw his uncle's petite Polynesian wife, Ashley. It was the third marriage for Sonny and seemed to be his happiest.

"Hey, Ashley."

She smiled at him, flipping her long raven hair off her shoulder. "You have a visitor."

"Oh?" Keanu met her eyes. "Who?"

"He's waiting in the living room."

Keanu excused himself while thinking: *I'd love to play host to Raquel. Bet the place would impress her, though I'd rather be the one to pique her interest more.*

He strolled across the eucalyptus hardwood floor and rounded the corner before spotting a familiar face. Victor Flint was his college dorm roommate and probably the only friend Keanu had kept in contact with over the years on the islands.

"What's up, dude?" Victor beamed, moving toward him.

Keanu sized up the man who was two inches shorter and a shade darker, with a slender build and black cornrows in front and micro braids in back. He gave him a hug. "I'm good."

"Heard you were back in town," Victor said. "Thought I'd come over and see for myself."

"Yeah, I'm pretty much home to stay," Keanu told him. "I was going to call you."

"Now you don't have to. Why don't I take you out to one of the hottest clubs in Honolulu with drinks on me? We can catch up."

"Sounds like a plan, so long as you join us for some chow." Knowing his uncle, Keanu was sure he'd cooked more than enough to handle a guest at the table.

"Would love to."

Keanu had planned to lay low for a while with clubbing, trying to steer clear of the nighttime social scene that was responsible for at least part of his image problem. He was sure Raquel would suggest he find another outlet for entertainment. But since he was just hanging out with an old friend and not there to pick up women or get wasted, there was no reason to believe things would get out of hand and set him back a peg or two in his new mission.

Raquel stepped inside the Mango Bar, the most happening place these days in Honolulu. As expected, it was packed with locals and tourists alike. That was one thing she loved about the islands, everyone knew how to let their hair down and have a good time.

How am I ever going to find Lauren in here?

No sooner had Raquel begun the search for her when she heard the recognizable voice say, "There you are, girlfriend."

Raquel looked to her right and saw her best friend, Lauren Newberg, approaching. "Been looking all over for you," she lied.

"So look no farther," Lauren said. "Here I am and ready to par-ty!"

Raquel smiled as she studied her petite friend. She had mid-length brown hair in textured layers and a side part, with matching brown eyes. She was wearing a coral spaghetti-strap fitted sheath and high heels.

"You look great," Raquel told her.

"Tell me something I don't know." Lauren flashed her teeth. "So do you."

"Just trying to keep up."

"Let's see if we can find a table and order some mai tais," Lauren suggested.

"Sounds good to me." Raquel followed her as they worked their way through the crowd. "I have some interesting news."

"Don't tell me you've met the man of your dreams at last?"

Under other circumstances that might have been a possibility. In this case, the man she'd met was off limits insofar as romance was concerned. "Not quite, but it does involve someone you are crazy about—"

"Is that who I think it is?" Lauren gushed suddenly.

"Who?" Raquel asked, following the flight of her gaze.

"Keanu Bailey!" Lauren put her hands to her mouth in disbelief. "It's definitely him and he's coming this way—"

Raquel gulped as she watched Keanu and another man practically part the sea while moving rapidly toward them. So much for Keanu getting a head start in cleaning up his partying image. At least he didn't have a woman on his arm. Raquel wondered just how long it would take for that to change as the evening wore on. Perhaps starting with Lauren.

"So we meet again," Keanu said, a wide grin playing on his lips as he gazed at Raquel.

"Hi, Keanu." She flushed while sizing him up. Unlike the sporty attire he wore earlier, Keanu was decked out in a stone blazer with a black polo beneath it, fog-colored khakis and dark bike-toe loafers. It made him look even better, if that was possible.

"You two know each other?" Lauren's mouth hung open as she stared at her friend.

"We met today," Raquel explained. "He's the person I was going to tell you about. Keanu has hired me as an image consultant."

"It's true," he confirmed, "and I'm sure Raquel will work her magic on me."

Raquel blushed at this obvious flirting on his part.

"This is my friend, Lauren Newberg," she introduced her. "She's one of your biggest fans."

"If not *the* biggest!" Lauren gushed, spreading her arms out for a hug.

Keanu offered a wide smile and fell into her arms, which Lauren quickly wrapped around him and didn't seem to want to let go.

He finally pulled away from her and gave an embarrassed little chuckle. "Nice meeting you, Lauren."

"You too," she cooed.

Keanu turned toward the other man. "This is Victor Flint. We go back a long ways."

"Hi, Victor." Raquel shook his hand while still pondering Lauren falling all over Keanu, who seemed to enjoy being pawed by her. Victor was slight in build with deep black eyes. She liked his cornrows, though she felt they would be all wrong for Keanu.

"Hey," Victor said as he shook Lauren's hand. He was clearly eyeing her and Keanu seemed amused, as if Victor had little chance with her.

"We were just headed to find a table," Lauren said, gazing at Keanu. "You're both more than welcome to join us."

"I'd like that," Keanu said quickly, turning to Raquel. "Assuming that we're not intruding?"

Actually, it was supposed to be ladies' night out, wasn't it? Or had that suddenly changed for her girlfriend who was obviously smitten by Keanu? As Raquel could clearly see that Lauren was all for the company, she could hardly be a party pooper and object. Besides, this would give her some additional time to check out Keanu as a client before coming up with a plan to revamp his image.

"Feel free to sit with us," she told him.

He grinned. "Great. And drinks are on me."

Keanu had expected this to be just another night out on the town. The best he could have hoped for was to run into Raquel, who was so fine he could hardly take his eyes off her. Keanu damned near wanted to give her a mouthwatering kiss right then and there. He might have, too, if Lauren wasn't sitting between them at the table, hardly taking her eyes off of him. She was cute, but not what he was looking for. Maybe she and Victor could get something going. He wondered if it was by design that Raquel had put some space between them, afraid of what they might be capable of if given half a chance.

"I really think you should reconsider retiring," Lauren told him, taking Keanu's attention momentarily away from Raquel. "The Pistons could really use you next year."

Keanu chuckled. It wasn't the first time he'd been told that his retirement was premature. But he'd put a lot of thought into it and had no desire to make a comeback. "They have some fresh young talent who will get their chance to shine now," he responded over his drink. "I'll always be a fan of the game, but I'm happy to step away and see what else I can do to give back for everything I've gotten out of life."

"You can't argue with that," Raquel said to her friend. "Keanu's still got a lot to offer in other ways, I'm sure."

"Hey, you're preaching to the choir," Lauren said. "Keanu is obviously an amazing man, both on and off the court."

"Yeah, the man can pretty much write his own ticket," Victor said. "Especially on his home turf."

"I don't know about that," Keanu said modestly. "I just want to fit in as best I can." He gazed at Raquel. "And with the island's best image consultant in my corner, I can't lose."

"Don't give me too much credit, too soon," Raquel said. "Let's just see how things go, okay?"

"Would you like to dance?" Keanu asked, wanting more than anything to feel her body next to his with the slow music just right.

Raquel hesitated and Lauren raised her hand as if in grade school. "If she doesn't, I'll be happy to show you some moves on the dance floor."

He smiled respectfully, but didn't want a substitute for the dance partner he preferred. "I'm sure you could," he said, "but I'd like to see what Raquel can do out there." He met her eyes. "So how about it?"

"You talked me into it," Raquel said, standing. "But just one dance. I don't want to hog all your time." She looked down at Lauren. "Especially if someone else wants a turn with you."

You can hog all my time if you want, baby. Keanu smiled and took her hand, leading her to the dance floor. He put his arm around the small of Raquel's back, drawing her close. As he imagined, they fit together perfectly.

"You smell good," he whispered in her ear. "What is that?"

"Thought you knew all the perfumes women wear," Raquel hummed.

"Not really. Many seem to be carbon copies of others."

"I think you're right about that." She rested her head on his chest. "It's Beyoncé Heat."

"A little Beyoncé in every bottle, huh?" He laughed deeply.

Raquel chuckled. "I suppose you could say that."

"The next time I run into Beyoncé, I'll thank her."

"Oh brag, brag, brag," quipped Raquel.

"It's no big deal," he assured her, holding her a little closer. "Believe me when I say she has absolutely nothing on you."

"Oh you think so, do you?"

Keanu grinned. "Just calling it like I see it."

"Are you always this smooth?" Raquel looked up at him. "Don't answer that. I think your track record speaks for itself. Yes, very smooth."

"Does that mean it's working on you?" Keanu met her gaze.

"Yes, no, I mean…don't confuse me," she stammered. "Look, I'm not interested in being wooed. Remember, we have a professional relationship—that's all."

He frowned. "Yeah, I hear you."

She stiffened in his arms. "Maybe we'd better end this now."

Keanu didn't release her. "At least let's finish the dance," he said, aroused at the thought of making love to her right on the dance floor. "I'll try not to cross any lines."

"Thank you." She continued slow dancing with him.

"So, are you seeing anyone?" Keanu asked after a moment or two. He imagined there was some lucky man in her life, given how beautiful and accomplished she was.

"Let's not go there," Raquel responded tersely.

"What—can't a guy ask an innocent, straightforward question in getting to know his new business associate?"

"I suppose," she said. "No, I'm not seeing anyone at the moment."

"Neither am I, if I haven't made that perfectly clear already," he told her, hoping she believed him.

"Well there's someone waiting over there at our table who seems pretty interested in changing that."

"I hadn't noticed." Maybe he had, but having fans attracted to him was par for the course, and he never reciprocated. Especially when his interest lay elsewhere.

"Yeah, right." Raquel rolled her eyes. "How could you not? She could barely take her eyes or hands off you."

He chuckled. "Sounding a little jealous there."

"Don't flatter yourself. Nothing to be jealous about."

"My sentiments precisely," he contended.

"Whatever the case, I think it's best that you leave her alone. Apart from working on a new and improved you, I wouldn't want Lauren brokenhearted."

"First of all, I'm not messing with her," Keanu stated. "And she won't be brokenhearted, as far as my position goes. I'm not attracted to Lauren that way, new or old me, trust me. Not compared to my attraction to you."

Raquel tilted her head back. "Here we go again."

"And where is that?"

"Trying to mix pleasure with business."

"Who says they have to mix?" Keanu spoke coolly,

near enough to kiss those inviting lips. "I have no problem separating the image consultant from the beautiful, sexy woman before me."

"Well, I do have a problem separating the handsome, sexy man you are from the client I'm working with." Raquel sighed. "I'm sorry, but that's just the way it is."

So she finds me sexy. That's good to know. "Don't be. I'm not. What's meant to be will be, and I don't think either of us could stop it even if we wanted to."

Raquel batted her lashes. "You're pretty full of yourself, aren't you?"

"Isn't that your job to help me get past that?" Keanu asked without blinking.

"Maybe to some degree. I'll see what I can do." The song ended and she pulled away from him. "I think we'd better join our friends."

Keanu wished they could have stayed in each other's warm arms all night, including moving on to the bedroom, where he imagined things would heat up in a hurry. But it wasn't in the cards this night.

"Good idea," he said.

In the ladies' room, Raquel had to dab some cold water on her face. But that did little to cool her body made red-hot from Keanu's touch on the dance floor, the way he looked at her as though able to see every inch of her, and the desire he had single-handedly managed to build up inside her like steam in a locomotive raring to come out. She wasn't used to having a man affect her that way. Clearly Keanu wasn't just any man. But he was her client and that had to be her number one priority, even if he seemed to be perfectly all right with making things very personal between them.

She heard the door open and Lauren stepped inside. "Are you all right?" she asked, a worried look on her face.

"I'm fine," Raquel said. "Just needed to apply a little makeup."

"I still can't get over the fact that Keanu Bailey is your client."

"Well, get over it. He's just another person who hired me to do a job."

"He's hardly 'just another person,'" Lauren begged to differ. "Who'll be next to grace your client list, Barack Obama?"

A smile lifted Raquel's cheeks. "After he retires from office, who knows."

"Unlike Barack, Keanu is here now and hotter than hot."

"Yes, that's true on both counts," Raquel admitted, but still refused to get too carried away with it. She wanted to temper her friend's enthusiasm as well, if for different reasons. "I didn't think he was your type."

"Think again," Lauren told her. "Just because I don't usually date men who look like Keanu Bailey, doesn't mean I can't."

He's also a man who's not into you, if I'm to believe him. "Maybe you shouldn't get too wrapped up in Keanu."

"And why not?" Lauren stared at her. "Let me guess: you want him for yourself?"

"No, that's not it," Raquel insisted. "I just don't want to see you get hurt by falling for a celebrity athlete who—"

"Has his sights set on someone else…"

Raquel met her eyes. "I didn't say that."

"You didn't have to," Lauren stated. "I'm not blind. I can see that Keanu is attracted to you—no matter what your position is on the subject."

Raquel tried to downplay it. "He's into all women." His history spoke for itself and she doubted that had changed. At least not overnight.

"Maybe once upon a time," Lauren said. "But right now, I honestly think he's hoping to make an impression on you over and beyond being a client."

"I've already set some boundaries," Raquel said, "that I expect him to abide by."

"Boundaries are made to be broken—maybe by the one making them. Loosen up a little, girlfriend. Nothing says pleasure and business can't mix, if it's the right combination."

"And you're okay with that?" Raquel asked her. She certainly didn't want a guy coming between their friendship. Especially not a high-profile client.

Lauren paused. "Sure, why not? If I can't hook up with him, no reason why you shouldn't date the most eligible male on the islands. That won't stop me from continuing to be his number one fan."

Raquel didn't doubt that for one moment, which was part of the problem. She was sure that Keanu had many such dedicated fans. Competing with them for his attention and ego wasn't a road she really wanted to go down.

"Think I'll stick to working with him for the time being," she said.

"We both know he's definitely your type," Lauren said as she powdered her nose. "So why fight it?"

"I'm not denying that," Raquel told her and applied

some lip gloss. "Just the timing and baggage he carries as an athlete isn't for me."

Lauren scoffed. "We all carry some baggage. Don't let that stand in your way."

How could she not? If she were to play with Keanu's fire, she would almost certainly get burned.

"We'll see what happens," she said evasively. "Right now he's my client and I intend to earn my keep."

"Fine, I give up," Lauren said. "If you want to leave the man hanging, that's your call."

"I'm sure he'll get over it quickly enough." Raquel wouldn't be too surprised if he'd already found another attractive lady out there to occupy his attention. "Anyway, enough about us. What do you think of Victor?"

"There's some possibilities there," she hinted. "He's nice on the eyes too, has his own business and seems to think I'm just what he's looking for. I gave him my number. If he calls, he can take me out to dinner. If not, oh well…"

"Hope it works out." No reason why one of them couldn't hit the jackpot romantically, even if Lauren would obviously have preferred Keanu as her first choice. "We'd better get back before Victor wonders where you are."

Lauren fluttered her lashes. "Uh, don't you mean before Keanu wonders where his image consultant has gone?"

Raquel smiled, not wishing to be drawn into that trap. Keanu would be Keanu whether she was there or not.

When they went back into the bar, Raquel heard the disc jockey say, "I'd like to personally welcome back home—and I know you all feel the same way—one of Honolulu's star attractions. Give it up for NBA great Keanu Bailey."

The crowd cheered and Keanu seemed to lap it up as he went around shaking hands like a politician. Raquel could see that he was as popular as ever locally, which wasn't the issue. It was elsewhere that his image had taken a hit and needed some fixing. But would he truly be able to see the forest for the trees, when there were many people out there telling him they loved him just as he was?

Chapter 3

Early the next morning, Raquel was in the fitness center exercising on the elliptical machine for forty-five minutes before lifting weights. After a quick shower and breakfast, she spoke to a group of businessmen on leadership and communication skills. Back at her office, she worked on some ideas for Keanu to improve his image that she hoped to present to him this afternoon. She asked her assistant to get him on the phone.

I assume he didn't close the club down last night and is still in bed trying to recover. She had decided to leave a bit early, as he had been preoccupied with fans and Lauren had been caught up in sweet words from Victor. Up until then, Raquel had admittedly enjoyed Keanu's company more than she cared to admit. He had a way with words and was a real charmer. She imagined a girl could easily fall for him were her guard not up.

The phone buzzed, snapping her out of it.

"I have Mr. Bailey on the line," her assistant said.

"Mahalo." Raquel sucked in a breath while wondering what Keanu would have to say for himself. If anything. "Aloha *kakahiaka,* Keanu," she said, meaning good morning.

"Back at you," he responded. "Where did you disappear to last night?"

"I had to go home and prepare for a meeting this morning." That was at least partially true. "I thought a quiet exit might be best."

"I understand. Missed you all the same."

"Sure about that? Seems to me you had your hands full with doting fans." Including Lauren, though Victor seemed to have taken away some of that attention.

"I would have been happy to walk you out, fans or no," Keanu said.

"That wasn't necessary. I walked in all by myself and had no trouble leaving the same way."

He chuckled. "Quite the independent lady, aren't you?"

"Most of the time," she conceded, hoping it didn't come across as cold.

"That's cool. Nothing wrong with taking the reins and going with it in life."

"I agree. Anyway, I'm calling to see if we could meet for lunch and discuss ways to improve your image."

"I'm down with that," he agreed enthusiastically.

"Do you know where Tulips is?"

"Been there a couple of times," Keanu said.

"Good, I'll see you there at one," Raquel told him.

"Sounds fine."

She hung up and wondered if she'd really be able to

stick to developing just a professional relationship with him. She knew it wasn't smart to allow herself to feel something personal for a man who had been there, done that too many times for her comfort. It was sure to be in her best interests to keep things professional.

Half an hour later, Lauren phoned. "I spent the night with Victor," she said excitedly.

"Wow, that was quick," Raquel said with surprise, considering last night she seemed still half stuck on Keanu.

"What can I tell you—one thing led to another and that was that."

"No regrets the morning after?"

"None at all. The man is dynamite in bed and fun to be with."

"I'm happy for you—and him," Raquel said. "Guess it was a good thing we happened to run into Victor and Keanu at the club."

"Very good," Lauren said. "Speaking of, Keanu seemed pretty out of it from the moment he learned you'd left last night."

"It wasn't that big of a deal." Raquel found it hard to believe he would have given it much thought. "He was busy enough without my presence."

"Maybe, but you would've thought the man had just lost his best friend—or maybe future lover."

Raquel couldn't help but laugh at her friend's too-vivid imagination. "He didn't lose either. Keanu and I only met for the first time yesterday," she reminded her. "He certainly hasn't lost me as an image adviser. As for the rest, we'd best focus on what brought us together in the first place."

"So you keep saying," Lauren hummed.

"And meaning," Raquel said. "Don't go getting any wild ideas. Just because you and Victor hooked up doesn't mean that's in the cards for me and Keanu."

"Not saying a thing, girlfriend. What will be, will be."

"Exactly." Raquel could read between the lines, whether she agreed or not. Right now, she only wanted to cordially get through the luncheon meeting with Keanu and see where things went from there.

Keanu drove his car toward downtown Honolulu. He thought about last night and how one minute Raquel had disappeared into the ladies' room and practically the next she was gone after only a few words. Granted, he was momentarily distracted by fans wanting a piece of him, he would much rather to have spent more time socializing with Raquel, even if it was to be mostly shop talk per her wishes. Apparently she was put off by the star treatment he was getting. Either that or she remained intent on denying the sexual vibes between them.

Admittedly, he was used to getting women he went after. But Raquel was anything but a run-of-the-mill woman. She was clearly her own person and probably as stubborn as him. Beneath that businesswomen exterior though, Keanu was certain there was a sexual, sensual, loving lady just waiting to be brought to the surface. He intended to be the man to do that, whether she realized it or not.

But business came first. Or so Raquel would have him believe. It was all for the good of improving an image that Keanu felt still portrayed only his younger, more reckless self. There were times when he'd allowed his temper to get the better of him, but never in a malicious way. And he had been a bit reckless in carousing and going after famous women, if only for the challenge and mutual benefits. But that was old news. He wanted a new image that would reflect the mature Keanu he was now. Which he believed Raquel would help make happen. He owed it to himself to see this through and to give himself further inroads to promote his brand into retirement. That didn't mean he didn't still find the image consultant hot and well worth pursuing.

Keanu turned onto Alakea Street and saw the restaurant. After parking, he went inside. He immediately spotted Raquel sitting in a waiting area, typing on her BlackBerry. She looked up at him.

"Sorry, I'm a few minutes late," he told her. "I'd forgotten that the downtown traffic during lunch hour can be maddening."

"It's fine," she said, standing with a brown leather briefcase. "It gave me the chance to do a little business-related texting."

"Do you ever give yourself a break from business?" he asked.

She rolled her eyes. "I seem to recall that I did that just last night."

"Yeah, guess you did. Only not long enough."

"Sorry I had to cut the evening short," Raquel said as though she meant it. "I saw you were busy, so thought I would just slip away, knowing we would see each other soon enough."

"Right you were." Keanu could hardly argue with her rationale, even if he would've preferred her company over anyone else's last night. He gave her the once-over. Raquel had one of her power business suits on that only made her look sexier and more desirable. "Well, shall we go in?"

"Yes, let's." She smiled at him and Keanu smiled back with anticipation of the opportunity to spend more time together.

They sat by a window facing Merchant Street, not far from Kamehameha Statue, and ordered red wine while studying the menu.

"Any recommendations?" Keanu looked over his menu at Raquel, who had obviously been there more often than him.

"I'd try the coconut shrimp and grilled jumbo asparagus," she suggested.

"Sounds good to me."

"I'm going to go with the chicken satay skewers," Raquel said, "and the same side dish."

They ordered, and Keanu readied himself for her plan of action to turn his negative image into a positive one. "So what did you come up with?"

"Oh, a few things that I believe can definitely enhance your image as a retired and reformed ballplayer who still has a lot to offer not only your fans, but advertisers and merchandisers as well."

"I'm listening…" Keanu's interest was piqued as much for her business sense as for the woman herself.

Raquel set her briefcase on the table. "To start with, I think you need to improve your wardrobe."

He glanced down self-consciously at his attire: a customized black jersey, black with a white stripe fleece track pants and his black-gray sneakers, which he helped design. Lifting his eyes back up, Keanu cracked a half grin. "You have a problem with these clothes?"

Raquel smiled evenly. "Not at all. I love your sportswear, as I'm sure all basketball fans do. But now that you're shooting, so to speak, for a broader audience in the business world, you need to dress more conservatively. This is particularly true when meeting with executives and merchandisers who want to see not necessarily the athlete, but the retired player whose attire speaks of maturity and confidence." She opened the briefcase and removed some eight-by-ten photographs, passing them to Keanu. "These are some examples of what I'm talking about—"

He studied the pictures of thirty-something men who were well-dressed in expensive suits or business casual attire. Keanu saw nothing wrong with the clothing. But he'd always felt more at ease dressing in a laid-back fashion.

Apparently that would need to change.

"I get what you're saying," he told Raquel. "I'm sure I can spiff up my wardrobe."

"Good." She smiled at him. "Moving on…as a still very popular ex-basketball player, I believe that holding a free basketball camp for underprivileged children in Honolulu would be a great place to start your transformation. The local media loves reporting on these types of events."

"I've done basketball camps before," he pointed out.

"Yes, but not here and not without forcing kids to pay hundreds of dollars to attend, which was money that you didn't need."

"Good point." He smiled. "I like it."

"Excellent." She passed him some flyers. "I think the Honolulu Community Center would be a great place to hold the camp, but there are also several schools— including one you attended—that I am sure would be happy to contribute their basketball court and equipment. You might even want to donate a few pairs of your sneakers as part of the program."

Keanu glanced at the information. She was thorough, if nothing else. "Again, I like it."

"Next, I think you should set up a nonprofit foundation through which you can donate funds to other organizations such as the American Red Cross, American Cancer Society, American Diabetes Association, American Heart Association, you get the picture. Or use the foundation as a funding source for any individual charitable donations you choose to make. This is really a terrific way to give back and get your name out there as someone who cares about others and is willing to back it up through selfless contributions."

Raquel passed a few pamphlets across the table to that effect. Keanu was impressed with her attention to detail. He had wanted to put together a foundation for a long time, but between playing ball and making money through endorsements and investments, there never seemed to be enough time. Now there were no such excuses.

"I'd like to set up a nonprofit foundation," he agreed.

"Wonderful." Raquel smiled. "I've got some other great ideas as well."

"Looks like we'll have to put those on hold," Keanu said as he noticed the waiter coming with their food. He gathered up the materials that had been spread across the table and handed them back to Raquel to be retrieved later.

As much as he liked hearing what the image consultant in Raquel had to say, Keanu was keen on using this time to get to know more personal information about her. He knew next to nothing about what made her tick, yet wanted to know everything about her, one layer at a time. Or would she resist this as too intrusive for their professional involvement?

After tasting the coconut shrimp, Keanu cast his eyes upon Raquel's lovely face. "I feel like you have me at a disadvantage here."

She cocked a brow. "Do I? How so?"

"I hardly know much about the woman I've entrusted to help me out," he said. "Why don't you tell me something about yourself?"

Her face flushed. "All right. What would you like to know?"

What wouldn't I like to know is a better question. "How did you get into this business?" he asked, deliberately tackling something that seemed right up her alley.

She put her fork down. "I suppose you could say I got started in church when my mom began teaching other women social skills and etiquette after the service. I used to watch her and say to myself, 'I could do that someday.' I took that confidence into college with a dual business and communications major."

"Impressive," he hummed.

"Well, you asked."

"Indeed, and I'm glad I did." Keanu tasted his wine. "What do you do for fun, aside from being a pretty damned good dancer?"

Raquel's face brightened. "Funny you should mention that based on one slow dance at a club," she said.

"Guess one slow dance made a believer out of me," he said.

"Well, in fact, I love dancing. I'm actually a hula dancer on the side."

"You…a hula dancer?" Keanu's eyes widened. "I didn't see that one coming."

"Most people don't," she said with a little laugh. "I got into it by accident. A friend of mine hula dances, and one time she asked if I'd like to fill in for another dancer who didn't show up for a performance. I stepped in there, picked up a few routines, and loved it. The exercise is great and it's fun stepping outside my element to woo onlookers."

"I'll bet." The notion of Raquel shaking those hips left and right sent a streak of arousal through Keanu. He fought to suppress the feeling. "I look forward to seeing you perform sometime."

"I'm sure you would," she said demurely.

Keanu grabbed a wheat roll from a basket and nibbled on it. "Have you always lived in Hawaii?" he inquired.

"Ever since I was five," Raquel answered. "My dad was in the navy and we moved around a bit before he settled into the life of an officer in Honolulu."

"I see. So your parents still live here?"

A shadow crossed her face. "My dad died three years ago, but my mother is still here and doing well."

"Sorry to hear about your father." Keanu took a breath. "I lost both my parents years ago to a car accident. My uncle raised me and kept me on the straight and narrow."

"Guess we both have had to deal with some harsh realities in life," Raquel said sadly.

He nodded. "Yeah. It's made us who we are."

"True."

I like who you are and something tells me the feeling is mutual. "I'm surprised our paths have never crossed on the island," he told her, wishing they had before now.

Raquel chuckled. "Oh, really? I don't think we've traveled in the same circles."

Keanu raised an eyebrow. "And what circles do you think I travel in?"

"The celebrity circuit…where commoners usually aren't allowed unless the celebrity decides to come down to earth."

Keanu couldn't help but laugh at that. "You've got it all wrong, at least where I'm concerned. I admit that as an athlete, I've gotten caught up a little bit in stardom and all that comes with the territory. But deep down inside, I've always been that same average kid who grew up on the playgrounds of Honolulu."

"Excuse me, but I doubt that you've ever been *average,* Keanu," Raquel declared, and forked a piece of chicken.

He laughed again. "Well, maybe as you get to know me more, I can convince you otherwise."

She batted her lashes. "We'll see about that."

Keanu smiled as he poured more wine into their glasses.

Raquel tried to keep her mind on the purpose of their luncheon, but Keanu seemed determined to make that as difficult as possible with his incredible sex appeal and the way he looked at her. Yet she had to stay focused. She wanted to succeed in helping him become a new man in the business world. That meant putting any attraction she had for him on hold. At least for now.

"Let's talk about your partying and womanizing,"

she said bluntly, knowing this was apparently one of his greatest weaknesses.

Keanu tightened his shoulders defensively. "Do we have to?"

"I'm afraid so." She paused to sip water. "As for the partying, my recommendation would be for you to lay low for a while so the paparazzi won't continue to lie in wait for unflattering or risqué images that could set your progress back a few pegs."

"You're right, I'll have to put a lid on that. Not to say that I ever went quite as overboard as the press would have you believe."

"Be that as it may, I'm sure you well know, perception is everything."

"Yeah," he conceded with a nod. "Anyway, I'm getting too old for that kind of thing, so…"

"You're hardly over the hill," Raquel told him. Quite the contrary, he was the same age as most of the men she liked to date. But they weren't dating, and she wasn't about to encourage it.

"I suppose I'm still climbing up the hill," Keanu agreed. "I'll just have to leave the party animal at home."

"Good." She flashed a smile, satisfied that he was so accommodating to her recommendations thus far. Now all he had to do was follow through, which was always the hard part for her clients. There was one more item she had to toss at him.

"I know you've said that the womanizing is pretty much a thing of the past too," Raquel said, meeting Keanu's steady gaze. "But the proof is in the pudding. You'll want to try and steer clear of any type of drama or scandals involving celebrity women you've bedded or are thinking about bedding, or—"

"I'll definitely keep the ship moving in the right direction and avoid any icebergs of that variety," promised Keanu with his trademark grin.

"Sounds like you mean it."

"That's because I do. Besides, right now I only have my eyes on one beautiful woman and have no desire to look elsewhere...."

Raquel found his eyes locked on her face, causing her temperature to rise. The man was making it very hard, if not impossible, not to succumb to his obvious persuasive charms. *Do I really have that effect on him or is he just that good at winning women over?*

"Are we starting to cross that line in the sand here?" she asked herself as much as him.

"What if we are?" he asked.

"Business and pleasure still do not go very well."

"Now that depends on the business and the pleasure," Keanu offered suavely.

It's getting too hot in here for comfort. "I think it's time to go back to work for me," Raquel said, in case he got the wrong idea.

"That's cool. Let me walk you out."

Keanu left a generous tip, making Raquel wonder if he was trying to show off or if it was routine for someone who had money to burn. She decided it was likely the latter, as it was already obvious that she was taken with the former basketball player, both as a client and as an attractive, sexy man.

As with most afternoons on the island, it was sunny with temperatures in the low eighties. Raquel hoped it wasn't awkward once they got to her car.

"So, when do we meet again?" Keanu asked as Raquel pushed a button on her key fob to unlock her car.

"In a hurry, are we?" she teased him.

"Can you blame me?" His gaze never left her face.

Raquel scratched her cheek. "You're too much."

"Not more than you can handle, I promise."

Her eyes widened as his words conjured up sexual thoughts. Had he meant for that to be the case? Or was it just her overactive imagination?

"I'll keep that in mind." She paused. "Why don't you begin implementing some of the things we discussed and let me know how it goes?"

"I can do that," he said in a serious tone. "I still want to see you again—sooner than later."

"You will," she promised, surprised to realize that she meant it.

Keanu tilted his head perfectly and went for her lips. At the last moment, Raquel snapped her head back so his mouth fell short of the mark.

"What do you think you're doing?" she asked, though it was quite obvious.

"Thought a kiss might be a nice way to wrap up the luncheon," he answered simply.

"Well you thought wrong. This wasn't a date, in case you've forgotten." How could he have?

"I haven't. But it felt right to me. Obviously it didn't to you."

Raquel frowned. "Do you kiss all of the people who work for you?" she challenged him.

"Only the beautiful and spunky ones who have very kissable lips—who happen to live in Honolulu and help people like me to get my act together."

She watched the amused grin on his face. "This isn't funny. If you really want to work together, we have to keep the personal feelings out of it. Do you think you can do that?"

His brows knitted. "Yeah, if that's really the way you want it to be."

It wasn't what Raquel wanted, but it was what she believed was appropriate as she worked with him. "Yes, it is."

"Then so be it," he said concisely. "My mistake. I'll try to keep my lips to myself from this point on."

"Mahalo," Raquel said, while wondering if that was possible, given his nature as a man used to getting his way with women, no matter who they were. She didn't intend to be just another notch on the belt, something he should get used to. She got into her car and told him simply, "I'll see you later."

Keanu watched as Raquel drove off. He was amused by her resistance to the sexual attraction between them, even if he completely understood her desire to hold her ground as a professional. The woman definitely caused his blood to run hot and she was worth the pursuit, both in terms of intimacy and intellectual satisfaction. They had a platform to build something special on and he wasn't about to let it slide. Not when she had so much going for her, not the least of which was a willingness to work with him as a businessman. Next he had to get her to see that he had more to offer than she realized.

Keanu headed to his car and pulled out his cell phone along the way. He called Richard Brock, feeling he owed him an update.

"Hello, Keanu," Richard said. "I had you on my call list."

"I beat you to the punch. I just wanted to thank you for hooking me up with Raquel Deneuve."

"Glad to hear that's working out."

"Yeah, it is," Keanu told him. "The lady really knows her stuff."

"Which is exactly why I thought you should talk to her," Richard said.

"I know I can count on you to look after my best interests, even with my NBA career over."

"Of course you can," Richard said. "I'm still your agent and always will be as long as you need me."

Keanu arrived at his car. "I appreciate that."

"As far as your earning capacity, it can go on long after your basketball playing days are over, if you play your cards right. And teaming up with Raquel Deneuve is certainly a smart move."

"I know that." In more ways than one. Keanu thought about their near-kiss. He slipped on his sunglasses. "I plan to start a nonprofit foundation."

"Great idea."

"Wish I could take credit for it," said Keanu. "It was one of Raquel's ideas for putting a positive spin on my image."

"I'll be happy to help you set it up," Richard said.

"Thanks. I'll have my lawyer get in touch with you. We can have a conference call to set things in motion."

Keanu started up the car and drove off. He had a good feeling that his life after the NBA had a definite upside to it. Starting with a lovely lady by the name of Raquel Deneuve.

Chapter 4

Two weeks later, Raquel ran into her friend and fellow hula dancer, Kym Ogtong, outside her office building. The thirty-one-year-old Filipino had introduced her to the hula and, along with her husband, Peter, she toured the state and other parts of the country doing pair routines on the stage.

"Aloha." Raquel gave her friend a hug. "When did you get back in town?"

"Last night," Kym said.

"So how did it go?" Raquel asked, knowing that Kym and Peter had performed in Maui.

"Went great. Got a good workout and gave the tourists their money's worth."

"You always do, girl."

"Couldn't do it without Peter," Kym replied.

"I think it's more the other way around," suggested

Raquel, envious that they shared a love that allowed them to work and live together seamlessly.

"Mahalo. You know I feel the same way about you," Kym said. "We are two hot ladies at the luau."

Raquel beamed. "We do know how to burn up the stage," she admitted.

"Then you're coming tonight?" Kym asked.

"Of course. I wouldn't miss the chance to let my hair down and have some fun moving my body."

Kym smiled. "Same here. I'll see you then. I'm off to pay my father a visit and hope he lays off the lawyer talk—at least until I need to hire a multilingual corporate attorney or until Peter and I begin to make big bucks if that ever happens."

Raquel laughed. "Hey, at least you have him in your corner, just in case." What she wouldn't give to have her own dad back. It pained Raquel to think that he would never get to see her career jump in leaps and bounds. Or walk her down the aisle. Or maybe become a grandfather. Not to mention be there for her mother who was finally moving on, even if Raquel could not imagine anyone ever truly taking her father's place.

When she got back to her office, Raquel returned some calls and made a few others. It was all in an afternoon's work as a professional consultant. One person she resisted calling was Keanu. He hadn't called her either. Their last meeting ended on an awkward note when he tried to kiss her. Not a good idea when trying to build a professional relationship. But he didn't seem to get that and was obviously used to women falling all over him. Well, not this time. She refused to compromise her principles, even if the attraction was definitely there, along with the temptation to act on it.

Raquel took a breath, wanting to keep things in perspective and her eye on the ball. In spite of Keanu's personal interest in her, he did seem amenable to her ideas on executing a plan of action to improve his image. She needed to give him the space to do just that and not assume one attempted kiss had changed everything.

They were not Oahu's latest golden couple, no matter how much she secretly loved the idea. And they might never be anything other than client and consultant, although Raquel suspected Keanu was not the type to give up without a fight.

Keanu shot the ball from beyond the three-point line and watched it swish through, barely even hitting the net. Never mind that a hand was in his face all the while. He was playing in a pickup game at his old high school and having fun rather than being the fierce competitor that he had been in the pros, sometimes at the expense of his team and wallet. He ran down the court with the other players, and, when one slender teenager young enough to be his son tried to get past him for a layup, Keanu recovered, swatting it away.

Wagging his finger teasingly, Keanu joked, "Get that stuff outta here."

But then when the determined youngster got the ball again, Keanu let him make the shot unscathed, allowing the boy to build up his confidence as others had done for him way back in the day. He even high-fived him and said, "Way to shoot over an old man, but one who can still keep up with you." At least in spurts.

When the game was over, Keanu was exhausted. Though he kept in shape through tennis, swimming and weight lifting, he knew how easy it was to get out of game shape even in the less than a month it had been since calling it quits as a professional player.

That didn't mean he wasn't in good enough shape to take Raquel to bed, were it to happen.

Right now that was Keanu's only fantasy. He was certain that he and Raquel would be great together. And it went beyond the sexual attraction. Unlike other women he had known, she came across as someone totally down to earth, not in awe of him, and unpretentious. At the same time, she was sophisticated, strong, and obviously able to hold her own with him in terms of business acumen and success.

Keanu also wanted to convince Raquel that he was damned serious about reforming his image, especially where it concerned womanizing. The last thing he wanted was for her to believe his primary interest in her was sex, no matter how amazing he imagined it would be. He wanted the complete package and wouldn't allow his powerful libido to derail it. He was determined to hold the line till the time was right.

After grabbing his gym bag, Keanu went to see the athletic director, John Tawatao. He was in his office, one that had been occupied by Keanu's uncle when John was a physical education staff member.

"Nice to see you back at your old stomping grounds, Keanu," John declared, giving him a sturdy handshake.

"Thanks." Keanu half grinned, studying the gray-haired, shorter man. "Sometimes it seems like I never left."

"In many ways, you haven't. Your aura of greatness remains with this school—right alongside your father's."

Keanu blushed. "Actually, I was hoping I could cash in some of those chips."

"Sure, anything," John said. "What can I do for you?"

"I was thinking about conducting a basketball camp for underprivileged children," Keanu said. "In fact, maybe a few camps in the coming months around the island."

"That's a fantastic idea."

"I'd like to use the gym here to get it going and see if I can't inspire some local youth to develop their skills to become tomorrow's Keanu Bailey."

John's eyes crinkled as he smiled. "Say no more. I'm sure we can accommodate your request. It would be good for the school, the community and, most importantly, the kids who all want to be like Keanu."

"It'll be just as good for me," Keanu assured him, thinking about how it would surely put a smile on Raquel's beautiful face. He only wished he had put this into motion on his home turf much sooner, giving hope to a new generation of would-be athletes. The important thing was that he was giving something back now, while showing all who were watching that he was ready to turn over a new leaf and become a better role model.

As always, Raquel was a bundle of nerves and anticipation as she prepared to go on stage with the other hula dancers for the song and dance extravaganza at the Seaside Luau. Her costume consisted of a traditional pa'u, or wrap skirt made of tapa, and a matching bikini top, exposing her midriff, and lei formed from orchids as a headpiece, necklace, bracelet and anklet. Raquel's long hair fell onto her bare shoulders and she was barefoot. She watched from behind the curtain as fire knife dancers, including Kym and Peter, wooed the audience with a mesmerizing routine that embodied dances and songs of Hawaii, Samoa and Tahiti and included a death-defying performance of twirling knives of fire.

When they finished performing, it was time for Raquel and the other hula dancers to strut out on stage and do their thing to a captive group of tourists and locals. She took her place and, once the music began, Raquel started to move her hips and arms rhythmically. She stepped forward, spun around, went this way and that, in step with the choreographed moves that she had down pat after so many performances. The audience clapped enthusiastically.

This gave Raquel a warm feeling. She put a big toothy smile on her face, happy they appreciated the performance.

That comfort level took a hit when Raquel's eyes suddenly landed squarely on Keanu's face. He was sitting at a table near the stage, openly staring at her.

Sitting back in his chair, Keanu was absolutely riveted with Raquel as she swayed her gorgeous body back and forth to traditional Hawaiian music. He was seeing her in a whole new light and loved every moment of it. What he wouldn't give to have a private performance from Raquel—one that went from seductive dancing to passionate lovemaking. With her long, muscular legs wrapped around his waist, he imagined them going at it all night and well into the next morning. The notion seared into his mind. He wanted nothing more than to see the dream turned into stark and delicious reality.

For the time being, Keanu would try to behave himself, because he needed Raquel the image consultant perhaps as much as Raquel the sexual woman. He wanted her to take him seriously on both fronts and was committed to that happening.

She seemed to meet his gaze for the first time and, aware of his presence, appeared to be unnerved momentarily before recovering and getting back into a smooth and sexy rhythm. He raised his Blue Hawaiian cocktail in a show of appreciation as Raquel and the other hula dancers finished their routines. After, they were joined by the fire dancers for a spectacular display of dancing, music and storytelling that left the audience breathless.

Before Keanu had settled down to witness Raquel and her fellow dancers do their magic, he had watched in awe as a Kalua pig was unearthed from the imu pit. He then proceeded to stuff himself silly with a luau feast fit for a retired basketball player. He'd dined on an all-you-can-eat buffet including cinnamon-spiced bananas, roasted pig, steamed white rice and coconut pudding, downing it with a tropical drink. Now he wanted to make up for filling his stomach with a good workout—though he doubted any type of workout could measure up to he and Raquel sweating profusely while working out in bed.

"What are you doing here?" Keanu heard Raquel's terse voice as he came back to the present.

"Aloha," he said, offering a broad smile while standing up.

"That didn't answer my question."

He noted that she was still in costume and looking as

sexy as hell with one hand resting on her hip. "I came to watch the show."

"You mean to watch me?" Raquel's eyes narrowed.

"That wasn't my intention. My uncle suggested I check out the hottest luau on the island. I had no idea this was where you did your thing."

She flashed him a skeptical look. "So how did you enjoy the show?"

"I loved it. You're actually very good."

Raquel blushed, softening. "It came with a lot of practice."

"I'm sure." He envisioned her practicing those sexy moves to perfection. "Nice to see your let-the-hair-down playful side."

"It gives me a good balance," she said.

"I'd say it gives you more than that. You seemed to be truly in your element up on stage."

Raquel tossed her hair. "I suppose so, as a side gig. I'm best in my business mode, though."

"What about your personal mode?" he tossed at her.

Her eyes widened. "What about it?"

"I would think that has to come first in your life."

"I don't really have much of a personal life these days, so maybe not so much right now."

Keanu cocked a brow. "We'll have to do something about that."

"I hesitate to ask what you've got in mind," she said suspiciously.

He had plenty in mind but did not want to frighten her off. "I was thinking that you could drop by my place tomorrow for a swim?" he suggested, as it was the first nonsexual thought to come to mind.

"A swim…?"

"Yes. You do swim?"

"That's pretty much a prerequisite when you grow up in Honolulu, don't you think?"

"Yeah, I do," he said. "But you never know."

Raquel gazed at him. "I suppose you have an Olympic-sized swimming pool?"

"Something like that," he admitted. "But don't worry, if you get in too deep I promise not to let you drown."

She chuckled. "Don't think you have to worry about that. I was on the swim team in high school and am pretty comfortable in the water—including the deep end."

"What aren't you good at?" Keanu said.

Raquel folded her arms. "Conversing while I'm still in costume half-naked."

He met her eyes and was sure she could read his raw desire, even though he was trying to contain it.

"In that case, you better go change," he told her.

"Don't wait around for me," she said. "After a performance, the group usually gets together for a drink and some evaluations."

"No problem." Keanu would have liked nothing better than to monopolize her time, but recognized that it wasn't the way to get to Raquel's heart. "I'll see you tomorrow—at three, if that's cool?"

"I'll have to do a little schedule juggling, but three is fine," she said. "Just so we're clear, this is to swim and not pick up where we left off a couple of weeks ago."

He smiled crookedly. "I promise, I won't make you do anything you don't want to do."

"Fine."

Keanu gave her a card with his address, but suspected she already knew the house's location, as it had been featured on local news programs and in national magazines as one of Honolulu's most impressive, energy-efficient homes.

"Have an aloha *ahiahi,*" he told her, meaning good evening.

"You too," Raquel replied.

"Who was that gorgeous hunk you were talking to?" Kym asked Raquel in the dressing room.

"A client of mine." Or was he more than that now that she had agreed to go swimming with him?

"I'm sure he thought you were fabulous as a hula dancer."

"He gave me kudos," Raquel admitted.

"I'll bet he did." Kym laughed. "Probably had him wishing he was more than just your client."

Raquel could hardly deny it, since Keanu had made that perfectly clear from the start. Seeing her hula dancing probably raised his level of interest a few notches. But she still wasn't ready to jump the gun on their relationship, even if the sparks were there. As far as she was concerned, they would continue to operate on the basis of a business relationship with some potential side benefits. Such as swimming.

"I'm not saying there aren't some possibilities there," she told her friend. "He's single, I'm single, good looking, both successful in our own rights, so..."

"So I say go for it," Kym declared.

"I try to stay away from dating clients." Especially ex-basketball players with a long track record of breaking women's hearts.

"Not all clients look like this one. Rules are made

to be broken. Maybe this is the time to toss those right out the window and see what he's made of."

"I already have a good idea of that," Raquel said. "He's an athlete. Need I say more?"

"Not all athletes are created equal," Kym pointed out. "If this one chose you to do business with that's already one indication that he might be a keeper."

Raquel laughed. "You have a point there."

"Seriously, you're entitled to set your sights on someone who's available—client or not—even if the last guy turned out to be a dud."

"Don't remind me." Raquel thought of Harrison Chamberlain as nothing more than a distant memory. They had dated for over a year, having met on a blind date. A Native Hawaiian and construction worker, he was handsome and charming in his own way. They got along well enough when things were going good in his life. But after getting laid off, he seemed perfectly willing to sponge off her instead of finding another job. It reached the point where they fought more than they had civilized conversations and she realized it was time to move on without him.

Keanu was much more her type in terms of success, confidence and character. But was he really through with his party-hardy days? Or could his image-building be merely a smoke screen for more bad behavior?

"Forget I ever mentioned it," Kym said with a chuckle.

"Consider it—or him—forgotten," Raquel said, having changed back into her own clothes.

"I have a small favor I'd like to ask you." Kym looked serious.

"Okay…"

"Peter and I have a one-day gig at a hotel in Kauai early next month. We thought it would be nice if we added another person. I immediately thought of you."

Raquel was flattered. "I don't fire dance," she reminded her.

"Don't worry, you won't have to do that," promised Kym. "You and I will hula dance and Peter will do the fire dance by himself. Please say yes. It'll be fun, really."

Raquel was considering it without looking at her schedule, which was often booked for weeks in advance. But she liked Kym and didn't want to disappoint her. "One day, huh?"

"Yes. Transportation and accommodations are covered and, of course, you'll be paid to perform."

"What day is the show?"

Kym told her that it fell on a Friday. "Let me just check to make sure I don't have anything going on that day," she told her. "If not, I'd love to take my hula dancing act to Kauai."

"Wonderful," Kym said. "And if you want to bring a friend along—or even a new client boyfriend—be my guest."

Raquel smiled thoughtfully. "I'll keep that in mind." She liked the thought of going on a romantic overnighter with a caring, ultra-romantic guy. It was premature to think that could be Keanu. But she couldn't help picturing them snuggled up in a hotel bed together.

Chapter 5

The next morning, Raquel cleared her schedule and went shopping with Lauren at the Aloha Tower Marketplace on Honolulu Harbor's pier, in search of a new swimsuit. She convinced herself that the shopping was just a treat for herself and had nothing to do with her newest client.

"What happened to all those swimsuits you had?" Lauren asked as they stepped inside the store.

"I still have them," Raquel said. "But I wanted something new."

"For whom?" Lauren's eyes widened. "Let me guess, does his first name begin with a *K* and his last name end with a *Y?*"

Raquel saw no reason to deny it, as Lauren would likely find out from Victor anyway. "Yes, Keanu invited me over for a swim. Since I love to swim, I figured why not?"

Lauren grinned mischievously. "Just a swim?"

"That's all there is to it," Raquel insisted.

"Yeah, right. Like I believe that. Especially when Keanu happens to be one of the city's most eligible— and too hot for words—bachelors."

Raquel twisted her lips into a pout. "Don't read too much into this. Keanu's a great and gorgeous guy. But right now we're still just client and image consultant. They will always come first so long as I'm in his employ. If something happens beyond that, we'll have to see how it goes."

"Well, there's no better way to establish that something than playing footsies in the water at his mansion," Lauren said with clear envy.

"I'm not after his money," Raquel said as they approached some designer swimwear. "I think I'm doing fine with my own career and finances, thank you."

"Don't get defensive, girlfriend. It is what it is. The man's swimming in dough and he's got his eye on you. As your best friend and his top fan, I say enjoy hanging out with him and whatever happens, happens."

"Okay." Raquel planned to enjoy herself without thinking too far ahead. "Now enough of that. Help me find the perfect bathing suit."

"I think I may have found just that," declared Lauren. She lifted up a polka-dot-print bikini so skimpy that it left absolutely nothing to the imagination.

"Please," Raquel groaned. "That's just not me." At least not for a swim date, if she could call it that.

Lauren frowned. "Then what is?"

Raquel spied a swimsuit that was more her style. It was a maroon ruched one-piece bathing suit that wasn't too revealing but sexy nonetheless. She held it up to her body. Perfect.

"What do you think?" she asked Lauren.

"I like it," Lauren said. "You're sure to cast a spell on Keanu with that on your already amazing body. I assume that's your plan?"

"Not exactly." Raquel draped the swimsuit across her arm. "I just want to wear something I'm comfortable in and have some fun."

"That's cool." Lauren continued browsing at the swimwear. "Now that I have reeled in Victor, I need something tantalizing to keep him wanting more."

Raquel smiled. She was pretty sure Lauren was doing her part to keep Victor engaged even without a swimsuit that would likely just be removed quickly. It made her wonder if things might eventually be headed that way with Keanu. The thought caused a ripple of desire to shoot through her. She stifled it and forced herself to approach this as an afternoon get-together in the pool with no expectations. After all, she had set the ground rules in advance.

She recalled Kym's words. *Rules are made to be broken.* But should they be?

"Let's see what we can find for you that will stop Victor in his tracks," Raquel told Lauren.

Raquel drove down Kahala Avenue alongside the ocean and not far from Diamond Head, the volcanic cinder cone known the world over. Kahala had some of the most desirable real estate in Honolulu and had been a popular location for Hollywood productions such as *Hawaii Five-O* and *Magnum, P.I.* She had seen pictures of Keanu's house. It was spectacular and left her mouth agape with envy. Of course, seeing it in a magazine could not compare to an in-person tour by the owner himself.

Hold on. I'm going there to swim, not to drool over his property, no matter how incredible it may be.

But, then again, the property was a reflection of its owner. If he wanted her to see his house, she would be delighted to do so.

The gate was open when Raquel arrived. Assuming that was for her benefit, she drove through and down a cobblestone driveway to the house. Keanu was waiting there beside his car, a cute grin lifting his cheeks.

Raquel had to trust that her appearance was up to par, and chose not to do any last-second primping with Keanu watching her every move. She got out of the car and grabbed her bag.

"Aloha," he said deeply.

"Aloha."

"Right on time, I see."

"Were you expecting me to be fashionably late?" she joked.

"Not at all." Keanu chuckled. "But sometimes traffic can be stalled by the tourists who are trying to see where the rich and famous live."

"I don't think I ran into any of those types." Raquel gave her own little laugh, not including herself as an occasional starstruck tourist. With Keanu it was less about the wealthy ex-athlete and more about the man she thought he could be.

He walked up to her wearing a Lakers T-shirt and cargo shorts. She inhaled his woodsy cologne.

"Did you bring your bathing suit?" he asked.

"Of course. That is why I'm here, remember?"

Raquel smiled. "Hope you're wearing something other than that in the water." Admittedly she was dying to see more of that athletic body in swim trunks.

"Absolutely," Keanu said with a confident half grin. "But first let's go inside and I'll give you the grand tour."

"I'd love to see it," she said.

Raquel followed him past the main entrance and into the sprawling mansion, which had windows at every turn offering panoramic ocean views. It had vaulted ceilings, cherrywood chair rails and a combo of hard-wood and limestone flooring. The living area opened up to a courtyard and the pool, and there seemed to be plasma televisions hanging on walls in every room. She stepped onto a covered lanai with cedar-wrapped posts in stone bases and polished travertine.

"Very nice," Raquel said. They were back inside and had barely gotten started with the tour. She could only imagine what else lay around the corner and upstairs.

"Yeah, it's pretty comfortable," Keanu said proudly.

They approached an older African-American man and a Polynesian woman who were coming down an elegant curved staircase.

"And who have we here?" the man asked.

"Unc, this is Raquel," Keanu responded. "She's my image consultant." He faced Raquel. "This is my Uncle Sonny and his wife, Ashley."

"Nice to meet you both," Raquel said with a smile. She could certainly see the resemblance between Sonny and Keanu.

"You too," Sonny said.

"Aloha," Ashley said.

"Aloha," returned Raquel.

"I was just giving her the grand tour," Keanu told them.

"Hope your shoes are comfortable for walking in," Sonny kidded. "It takes a while to go through this massive place."

"I'm beginning to see that," Raquel said, glad she had worn her flats.

"Would you like something to drink?" asked Ashley. "We probably have just anything you want."

"No, I'm fine, thanks," she replied.

"If you change your mind, I'm sure Keanu will be happy to show you where everything is in the kitchen."

"We're stepping out for a bit," Sonny informed Keanu. "There's a movie Ashley's been dying to see."

"Cool," he said. "Have fun."

"Always do," his uncle said. He looked at Raquel, grinning. "I'm sure we'll see you again."

"I hope so," she said, not wanting to appear too presumptuous. She watched as they walked away then turned to Keanu. "They seem nice."

"They are," he said. "Unc's always been a hard-nosed, no-nonsense kind of guy, but he's become mellower since Ashley came into his life."

"Guess that's a good thing."

Keanu nodded. "Yeah, I think he's at that stage of his life where he should sit back and smell the roses. Or eat popcorn at the movies."

Raquel smiled. It was clear that his uncle was special to Keanu, just as Raquel's mother was to her. She wondered if the new man in her mother's life would make her happier than she'd been since her father had died.

"Shall we continue the tour?" she asked Keanu.

"Got a better idea," he said with a lilt in his voice.

"Why don't we do that later and instead hop in the pool?"

Raquel met his amazing eyes. "Ready to get wet, are you?" she teased.

He grinned desirously. "Yeah, I could go for a good swim about now."

"Then let's go for it."

Keanu led Raquel to a huge downstairs bathroom to change, leaving her alone to marvel at it. With a sweeping glance past gleaming natural stone sinks and ceramic countertops and flooring, her eyes rested on a Jacuzzi tub. *Maybe I'll get to try that out for size someday.* Dream on. She turned her focus to removing her clothes and putting on the new swimsuit.

Wonder if he'll like it.

Glancing at her reflection in the mirror, Raquel doubted that would be a problem. She had been told often enough how heads turned when men saw her figure in a swimsuit. She usually took it in stride, but appreciated it nonetheless. Not that she was intentionally trying to turn Keanu on. But there was no reason either to shy away from opening up to him more and seeing where it went, so long as they were able to maintain their professional relationship as well. He certainly seemed to think so.

The moment she stepped outside the bathroom, Raquel's heart skipped a beat as she looked at Keanu, wearing a charcoal-colored Speedo swimsuit. Looking like a dark-skinned warrior, his biceps and quadriceps bulged with muscles, and he had an impressive six-pack. Intricate tattoos on both upper arms expressed his bad-boy side. She gulped, aroused, and centered her attention on his handsome face.

"Ready to take that dip in the pool?" he asked, grinning. *Yes, if only to cool off.* "Ready if you are."

Keanu's mouth dropped at the sight of Raquel in a swimsuit that clung to every contour of her marvelous body. He loved her shapely legs. To say nothing for her beautiful face surrounded by luscious hair that he was dying to run his hands through. He would love to take her right there on the spot. He might have gone for it in the past—indeed, definitely would have used his charms to seduce her. But he had given Raquel his word not to make any moves on her during this visit, hard as it was to live up to that. And if he was at all to convince her he had turned over a new leaf, Keanu knew he had to keep the libido in check.

He led her out into the courtyard. A full-sized basketball court was to the right. "There's an entrance to a secluded beach over there," he said, pointing. "We can check it out later if you like."

"I would like," she said gleefully. "I love the idea of a private beach."

Keanu imagined them making love in the sand with the ocean's waves cascading across their naked bodies. *There you are at it again, being driven crazy with lust for this beautiful woman. Cool it.*

They walked past the spa and toward a ten-foot glass-tiled infinity pool that included a forty-foot lap pool below and breathtaking ocean views. Keanu was eager to lower his body temperature, and dove right in. A moment later he heard Raquel splash into the pool.

"Hi," he said.

"Hey," she murmured, clearing her eyes of water. "It's great in here."

He swam over to her. "Yes, it is."

After a few minutes of swimming, Raquel surprised Keanu by splashing water at him. "Take that!" she teased.

He ran a hand across his face and grinned, enjoying this playful side of her. "Looking for a water fight, are you?"

"You'd have to catch me first!"

"And what do I get when I accomplish that?"

"Guess you have to find out," she told him.

With that, Raquel began to swim away, breaking into a butterfly stroke. Keanu watched with amusement, happy to give her a head start before catching up to claim his prize.

When he finally pulled even with her, Keanu wrapped his arms around Raquel, enjoying the feel of their wet bodies together. He tickled her.

"Let me go." She giggled.

"Can't," he told her. "I'm having too much fun." He tickled her again.

Raquel laughed hysterically. "Two can play that game, mister." She turned around and began to tickle him.

Keanu leaned his head back and laughed along with Raquel.

He realized this seemed the perfect time to kiss her. But would she balk? Accuse him of taking advantage of the situation?

It was a chance he was willing to take, trusting his own instincts combined with an overpowering need to feel those luscious lips upon his.

He tilted his head and brought their mouths together. She had soft, supple lips that were a perfect match for his.

Being a gentleman and wanting to be sure she was totally on board, Keanu parted their mouths and looked into her eyes. "You're a great kisser."

She met his gaze. "Is that why you stopped?"

He moved his legs in the water. "I don't want you to think I got you over here under false pretenses."

"I don't," she said. "Why don't we just go with the flow and see what happens?"

He smiled. "Yeah, why don't we."

Keanu was delighted to see that Raquel had let down her guard and opened herself up to the possibility of an intimate connection. He intended to make sure she didn't regret it for one moment.

He cupped her cheeks and kissed her again. She fell easily into the kiss, attacking his mouth with equal abandon. He put his tongue in her open mouth and relished her taste, becoming more aroused by the moment. Keanu could easily have kissed her nonstop, but he had a better place in mind for this.

"How about if we continue this in the spa?"

She paused. "The spa, huh?"

"Might be a bit more soothing," he suggested.

Raquel smiled. "So let's try the spa."

A minute later they had eased into the terra stone spa and stretched out on the full-body lounge.

"Now where were we?" he spoke lowly.

"You tell me," Raquel cooed.

His eyes lowered to her waiting mouth. "How about I show you?"

"Why don't you do that?"

Keanu grabbed her waist and pulled Raquel up to

him. He resumed the kiss and she gave it back to him. It felt so natural to have their mouths sucking one another's. He could only think about taking this to the next level. The way they were kissing, Keanu suspected Raquel was on the same wavelength.

Raquel had not been disappointed in the least with the kiss or the man. She hadn't expected their swim to be cut short, but neither of them could very well turn their backs on the sexual attraction that had been brewing, as much as she had tried to deny it. They continued to kiss as though they'd been doing so for years. Her breasts heaved and Raquel felt her nipples tingling like crazy. She could not remember a time when a man's kiss had aroused her so.

And clearly Keanu was experiencing a similar carnal reaction. With her leg wound around his below the pulsating water, she could feel his erection just begging to be let out of his swim briefs. Only this wasn't the time or place for that. Was it? And should they be moving in that direction so quickly?

They were practically making love in the spa right now, which was a bit too brazen for Raquel, no matter how good it felt. She pried their mouths apart from the kiss.

"Maybe this isn't such a good idea," Raquel said.

He touched her wet hair. "Or maybe it's a great idea?"

"We should slow down," she said.

"Why should we?" Keanu said. "Don't we deserve to play this out and let our feelings guide us?"

Raquel's body screamed yes, but her mind was still leery about going down that path. After all, they were still doing business together. And this was *anything* but business. She wouldn't want to damage that in any way.

But looking in Keanu's eyes, the only damage Raquel could see at the moment was denying the desire that they both needed to satiate in the worst way.

"Yes, I think so," she conceded longingly.

He gave her a toe-curling kiss. "I want to make love to you."

Raquel arched a brow. "Here?"

"Somewhere more appropriate for enjoying each other's company," he said.

She paused, debating if having sex with him was truly the right move to make at this point. She knew there would be no turning back once it happened. Again, Raquel's body spoke for her, needing to have this man inside her, giving her the satisfaction she knew he could bring her. They would simply deal with anything else as it came.

"So let's go to that appropriate place and be together," she whispered.

The scorching desire on Keanu's face told Raquel she would not need to tell him twice.

Chapter 6

Raquel entered the master bedroom in the east wing of the estate. It was palatial, with a split level that veered off into a large reading room and bathroom, with breathtaking views courtesy of wall-to-wall windows. The furnishings were stylish and dark. Raquel honed in on the king leather bed, and her mouth watered with eagerness over what was about to transpire there.

She gazed up at Keanu who was studying her body lasciviously as it clung to the wet swimsuit. He held her cheeks and began to kiss her again. She sucked on his lower lip and found her tongue entangled with his as the kiss deepened.

He massaged her breasts through the fabric of the swimsuit, rolling his fingers across the nipples, making Raquel want to shout in delight. Instead she let the hot kiss speak for her, and wrapped her arms around Keanu's neck.

They stayed that way seemingly forever before Keanu broke away. Staring yearningly into Raquel's eyes, he began peeling away her swimsuit, exposing her breasts and then her womanhood. Never taking her eyes off him, Raquel allowed the seduction to take place, wanting Keanu to see all he was getting. In turn, she wanted to see every inch of him as well.

As though reading her mind, Keanu stripped off his swimsuit and his erection sprang free. Raquel was taken with its sheer size, practically drooling at the prospect of his penis pleasuring her.

"I want to make you happy in every way," Keanu spoke with determination. He scooped her up in his sturdy arms and carried her to the bed.

Raquel was already trembling when Keanu ran his tongue across her tautened nipples, back and forth, and again, before peppering kisses down her stomach till reaching between her thighs. He put his face there and began kissing her.

"You taste very sweet," he murmured. "Sweeter than any wine."

She wasn't used to men who were interested in pleasing a woman that way and Raquel took delight in it. When Keanu's tongue started whipping across her core, she clutched his shoulders and cried out.

"That feels incredible," she said.

Raquel tossed her head back wildly as the surge of a powerful orgasm went through her veins. She thrust herself at his face shamelessly, wanting to hold nothing back. Keanu seemed to accept the challenge, placing a firm grip around her legs and licking her like crazy till Raquel couldn't take the torture anymore.

She moaned. "Oh…Keanu…it's happening."

"Let yourself go," he said. "It's all about you now."

Raquel took his words to heart as the ache between her legs built to a fevered pitch and another orgasm erupted. She sucked in a deep breath and quivered while the exultation gripped her. When it was over, she knew that it had only just begun. She needed far more from this man to make it complete.

"I want you inside me," her voice snapped. "I know you want it, too."

"Damned right," he said, "especially now that you're ready for me to have you."

She watched as he reached over and opened the drawer of an antique nightstand, removing a condom packet. He tore it open and put the latex over his erect manhood. Raquel braced herself for what she was sure would be the most intense sex she'd ever had, judging by what she had just experienced. It was as if carnal instincts had driven them to the edge of unchecked desire.

Keanu's lust for Raquel could not be denied. Seeing her like that on the bed, gorgeously naked, her body ripe for him turned him on to no end. Never before had he wanted a woman more.

He climbed onto the bed and brought his face down to Raquel's, and they kissed passionately. It was almost enough to cause Keanu to have an orgasm, but he wouldn't let that happen. Not till he was very deep inside her.

Breaking free of her swollen lips, he slowly entered her. Keanu held Raquel and thrust gently as she moaned with approval, urging him on. He kissed her face, ears, neck and breasts, taking the time to lick Raquel's nipples slowly and feeling her body react accordingly, before returning to her mouth with an all-out assault. His tongue worked its way inside the contours of her mouth, wanting to taste all of her.

Raquel wrapped her legs across his back and held on to Keanu's shoulders as he made love to her with an intensity and deliberation that had them both sweating. He felt her clamp down on him as if never wanting to let him escape her body. His arousal peaked. With his surge just moments away, he savored her, wanting to sustain their lovemaking for as long as possible.

"Don't stop," Raquel commanded, her nails clawing at Keanu's back.

He bit back the painful pleasure, wanting to accommodate her needs, which were obviously as powerful as his own. He adjusted his knees slightly to go even deeper inside her.

"Don't stop!" she wailed again.

"I won't, baby," he declared.

His shaft throbbed as he slid in and nearly out of her and back again, enjoying the passion of their locked bodies. When Raquel's body began to shake madly, it was clear to him that her climax was happening. At that point, his self-control began to wane and all Keanu could think about was letting go so they could reach those great heights of ecstasy together.

He let loose, guiding himself into her with a mission. Keanu grunted and Raquel allowed him in farther to help them both climb even higher in their quest for total fulfillment. They sucked on each other's lips voraciously and moved their bodies symmetrically till reaching the point of no return and all its glory.

When it was over, Keanu lay beside Raquel, catching his breath.

"Are you okay over there?" Raquel asked with a laugh.

Keanu grinned, eyeing her face with the afterglow of hot sex. "Couldn't be better."

"Just checking. Didn't want to wear you out."

He chuckled. "Never."

"The right words from a lover," she said.

Lover. He liked the sound of that. Even better was the anticipation of doing much more loving.

"I aim to please," he told her.

She ran her fingers across his chest. "Oh, you did, believe me."

He smiled. "The feeling is mutual. We make a great team."

Raquel batted her lashes. "Oh, do we?"

"Yeah, definitely." Keanu kissed her.

"Easy to say that when you've got me in your big bed, stark naked."

He chuckled. "True, but that doesn't change the facts. You are hot, with or without clothes."

"Well, mahalo."

Keanu kissed her again, this time a little longer. "Thank me all you want and I'll thank you back."

Raquel hummed as they kissed and abruptly broke away. "Can I ask you a little question?" There was a catch to her voice.

"Uh-oh…" He wondered what was on her mind. "Sure, go ahead."

"Did you really have an affair with Cassandra Tucker?" Raquel studied him.

Cassandra Tucker was one of Hollywood's hottest African-American actresses and was Emmy-nominated for her current television role as beautiful hotshot lawyer Loretta McClair. Keanu had met her at a star-studded event when he was with the Lakers.

"Cassandra can't hold a candle to you."

"That doesn't answer my question."

He met her gaze. "Why, are you jealous?"

"You wish," she said. "Just curious. I know there's been lots of rumors...."

Keanu would have preferred to leave it at that. But as he wanted to develop something serious between them, he didn't want to hold back on anything she wished to know about his past. Including the good, the bad and the regrettable.

"Cassandra and I had a thing going on for a while," he confessed.

"Meaning what?" Raquel asked.

"We were lovers."

She frowned. "Wasn't she married to Mitchell Malloy at the time?"

"They were separated," Keanu pointed out, "and he had been seeing someone as well at the time."

"That's supposed to make it all right?"

He tensed. "It was a long time ago."

"Not that long."

"What do you want me to say?" he said. "We made a connection and things just happened."

Raquel lifted her leg off his. "You mean like what just happened between us?"

Where is she going with this? "It's nothing like

what just happened with us. That was back when I was caught up in the Hollywood and sports lifestyle, right alongside Cassie. She was looking for something to keep her going and so was I. We did our thing and moved on."

"You see, that's what scares me about being in a relationship with a player," Raquel said. "It's too easy for you to 'do your thing and move on.'"

"That's not what's happening here," Keanu tried to assure her.

"How am I supposed to know that?"

"Because I'm not the same man now that I was then. And you're supposed to be helping me to get past those days. Or have you forgotten that?"

"Maybe I have forgotten by being in your bed," she tossed at him. "I'm not exactly doing my job by sleeping with a client and helping him to fall back into old patterns."

"That's ridiculous," Keanu said. "This isn't an old pattern, but a new one. You're the type of woman I want to be with, and I'm not about to apologize for that."

"And exactly what type of woman am I—one who gives in to feelings that the player in you can exploit?"

"It's not like that and you know it. We both went into this with our eyes wide open. Let's not allow my past with Cassandra Tucker or anyone else spoil what you and I have."

"We really don't have anything," Raquel said. "We had sex and that's it. It's my job to keep you on the straight and narrow. Not to give in to temptation and muddy the waters."

Keanu's nostrils flared. "So what are you saying?"

She sat up, covering her chest. "I'm saying this was

a mistake. We need to step back and focus on what you hired me for."

"Forget the damned image consultant for a minute," he said. "I'm not going to fire you because we slept together. Doesn't mean I want to go back to the way things were either. Not after what you and I just experienced. I doubt you do either, if you're honest about it."

Raquel sighed. "I'm being honest when I tell you that I don't want to rush into anything. I hope you can respect that."

Keanu felt as if he had been kicked in the gut. "I said before that I wouldn't want you to do anything you didn't want to. I still stand by that. I think we have a good thing going, but I can't make you get beyond my past indiscretions."

Raquel regarded him thoughtfully before sliding away from Keanu and off the bed. "I think I'd better go now."

"If you say so," he muttered, gazing at her nudity, even as she made a weak effort to hide it from him.

"I'll get my clothes and see myself out."

Keanu wanted nothing more than to get up and plead his case to her. But it seemed as though Raquel's mind was made up. He could only hope that once she settled down, they could resume what he saw as a promising relationship that could give them both what they had been lacking in each other. Or was that just his fantasy?

It had been nearly two weeks since things had turned sour between Raquel and Keanu and she'd left his house and bed fearful that she was only facilitating his womanizing. Maybe she had overreacted. Maybe not. She wasn't sure if slowing down their relationship, and pos-

sibly ending it, was the right thing to do. But she'd
freaked out in hearing Keanu confirm having an affair
with Cassandra Tucker. Though it was in the past, it
seemed to reaffirm the type of man Keanu had been
and could be again. She wasn't interested in falling for
someone who might one day leave her high and dry
when another attractive woman came along.

Was this her own insecurity at work? Or a defensive
mechanism that wasn't without merit? Maybe she owed
it to herself to stick to improving his image without getting involved with him romantically.

Raquel was in Chinatown picking up a few bargains
in a bustling open market. She had just completed a
coaching session with a group of executives, focusing
on growth-oriented performance and self-motivation.
Her mind wandered to Keanu and their hot sex. She
could still taste him on her lips. It turned her on even
as she tried to turn it off. Though she had enjoyed sex,
with Keanu things had admittedly reached a whole new
level of appreciation. He brought out the primordial instincts in her, leaving Raquel practically unable to con-
centrate on anything else.

But even with that realization, she was still reluctant
to have a repeat performance anytime soon, no matter
how great a match they were in bed. Neither she nor
Keanu had made any plans for future get-togethers,
and Raquel thought it might be best that way. She still
wasn't sure if they were meant to be a couple, even
though they'd had mind-blowing, body-twitching sex.
They were still doing business together, and she didn't
want that to take a backseat to a fling.

When she got home, Raquel put her items away
while thinking about inviting Keanu over for dinner

to try and smooth things over. There were still more things to talk about regarding improving his image. Perhaps a more relaxed setting would be a good thing for both of them to get back on the right track.

He's definitely not my typical client. I usually know where to draw the line between business and unbridled pleasure.

In this case, the lines were becoming increasingly blurred. Becoming involved with a celebrated athlete with a reputation for womanizing and partying was risky at best. And foolish at worst. But people did change, especially with the help of an image consultant. Maybe Keanu really did want to focus on one woman—her. He'd certainly done just that when he had given her his undivided attention when they'd made love. Shouldn't she give him the benefit of the doubt, for both their sakes?

The next day, Raquel was tidying up her apartment when the doorbell rang. She suspected it was Lauren. That was just like her to drop by unannounced. No doubt to snoop on how things were going with her basketball hero these days.

I'll just dodge the more intimate details, no matter how much she tries to coax out of me. Some things are better left private, even if Keanu and I have cooled off since the swim that ended up in his bedroom.

Opening the door, Raquel found her mother standing there. "Mom…"

"You were expecting someone else?"

"No," she said quickly. "If you'd called to let me know you were coming over—"

Davetta adjusted her glasses. "I was just in the neighborhood—at the bakery down the street—and thought I'd drop by for a few minutes."

Raquel resisted the urge to glance at her watch. "Come on in."

The moment her mother stepped inside, Raquel remembered she'd left the vacuum in the center of the living room.

"Don't mind that," she said.

"Are you sure you're not expecting anyone?" Davetta looked at her suspiciously.

"Lauren might drop by," Raquel suggested.

"Uh-huh," Davetta said skeptically.

Raquel rolled her eyes defensively. "What?"

"You don't usually get out the vacuum for Lauren. That means you've got other company coming over."

Raquel laughed. "You've got a devious mind, Mom."

"I'm your mother and I pick up on things," Davetta said, setting her purse down. "If you're trying to impress someone you've met, don't try and hide it."

She's right. Why should I hide it? Maybe because I don't want her to make a big deal out of it. I'm certainly trying not to.

"I'm not trying to impress anyone," she insisted. "The carpet needed to be vacuumed."

Davetta spotted a bottle of granite cleaner on the counter. "So this is all just for you, huh?"

I give up. She won't let it go till I say what she wants to hear. "All right, all right. I'm thinking about inviting a client over for dinner."

"Since when have you started inviting clients over for a home-cooked meal?" Davetta asked.

"This is the first time," she admitted.

"So who is he and why are you so secretive about it?"

"I didn't want you to read anything into a simple dinner and some wine."

Raquel leaned against a wall and sucked in a deep breath thoughtfully. "Keanu Bailey."

Davetta raised an eyebrow. "Not Keanu Bailey, the NBA superstar?"

"The same. He's hired me as a consultant."

"How nice." Davetta smiled. "The man's like royalty in Honolulu."

"I suppose," Raquel said, trying to downplay it. "He's also a human being like any of us with his own issues." Some of which she was helping him to resolve.

Davetta gazed at her. "Are you dating him?"

"No." *Wouldn't call a very steamy sexual encounter dating.* "Right now, we're just friends and business associates." Not necessarily in that order.

Davetta sat down on the chair. "But you obviously like him."

"Yes, I like him, Mom," Raquel said truthfully. "Doesn't mean we're ready to walk down the aisle and start having babies." *Why did I even say that when we're not even dating right now?*

"I never suggested that, though falling in love with a handsome multimillionaire athlete isn't such a bad thing."

Raquel sighed. *I knew I should have kept my big mouth shut.* "Now who said anything about love? And I sure don't need his money. I'm doing pretty well on my own," Raquel pointed out.

"I know that and I'm proud of what you've accomplished," Davetta said. "Doesn't mean if you're truly into each other you should simply turn away because of what he has."

"I'm not turning away from Keanu," retorted Raquel, feeling she could not win either way here. "We're not a couple. Far from it. Besides, with his history of womanizing, I'm not sure it would be too smart for any woman to get too attached to him. That includes one hired to try and clean up his act."

"I've heard all about Keanu's wild days. Men will always be men and sow their oats. But most men eventually settle down with one special woman who really does it for them. Maybe Keanu can see you as such a woman. Don't let fear stop you from throwing caution to the wind and giving this connection a chance to work."

"I'm not afraid," Raquel said, trying to convince herself. "As I said, we don't have anything serious going on other than my trying to improve his image. Right now, all I want is to invite him for dinner. I'm not even sure he'll accept." Things had been lukewarm at best between them since their last intimate encounter.

Davetta touched her glasses. "That's fine. Didn't mean to get you so riled."

"You didn't," Raquel said. "I just want to finish cleaning. So if there wasn't anything else you dropped by for—"

Davetta frowned. "All right, I get the message. I'll leave you alone." She rose.

Raquel hated to feel guilty about rushing her mother out. But it wasn't as though she were kicking her to the curb. They would have countless other times to see each other.

"I'll call you later."

"Actually, there was something on my mind—" Davetta said.

"What is it?"

"With Thanksgiving coming up, it's not too early to start thinking about dinner plans."

Raquel breathed a sigh of relief. "What type of plans?"

"Sean thought it might be nice for us to have Thanksgiving dinner together at his house," Davetta said. "I think it's a great idea and said I'd talk to you about it."

"I'm not sure I can commit to—" Raquel started, realizing it was more than a month away.

"Just think about it." Davetta got up. "If things have picked up between you and Keanu by then, you can even invite him. I'm sure Sean wouldn't mind, considering he's a huge basketball fan and would love to brag about Keanu actually being a guest at his house."

"I'll let you know," was all Raquel could promise. She wasn't about to commit to anything right now with her unpredictable schedule. Nor was she ready to invite Keanu to a Thanksgiving dinner when they were still trying to figure out what they meant to each other, if anything. As of now, they were just an image consultant and a retired athlete who had slept together once.

Maybe she could get better clarification once she invited him to dinner.

Keanu shot some hoops on his outdoor basketball court with his uncle. It was a good way for both of them to chill out and get a little exercise. Keanu made sure Sonny didn't overdo it, but knew he was in good shape for a man his age, which gave Keanu the motivation to also keep up with his own conditioning.

"So what's going on with that image consultant of yours?" Sonny asked as they played a game of horse.

Keanu frowned. He never could get anything past his uncle, who had seen him involved with many different women—some more serious than others. Instead of lecturing him, Sonny was always there to give advice or offer his constructive opinion. Unfortunately there wasn't much going on at the moment as Keanu had been giving Raquel the space she seemed to want, even though he badly desired to make this work between them. He tried not to let this detract from their professional relationship, which was still good—albeit largely confined to phone calls and text messaging.

"That bad, huh?" His uncle seemed to read Keanu's mind.

Keanu forced a little grin. "You know me too well."

"That I do." Sonny shot the ball, banking it off the backboard and into the hoop. "I assume the problem has nothing to do with her helping to reshape your image?"

"No, that's still very much on the front burner," Keanu said. He knew that Raquel was too much of a professional to allow their intimacy to get in the way of their business. He felt the same way. "We've talked about improving my wardrobe, doing a basketball camp and setting up a nonprofit foundation, among other things."

"Sounds like good stuff." Sonny tossed him the ball. "I'm glad that you're doing what you need to do in this new phase of your life."

"Yeah, I'm taking it seriously." Keanu shot the ball, swishing the net. He was ahead at H-O-R and hoping to seal the deal. "I think I can make an impact outside of pro ball."

"But the romance side of things has hit a snag?"

Keanu's lips pursed. "You could say that." He thought for the hundredth time about the slow seduction that had carried them from a fun and frolicking swim to his bedroom.

"I had a feeling it was something more than just business between you and the pretty lady."

"Not as much as I'd like it to be," Keanu admitted. "Seems like I'm having trouble shaking the past where it comes to winning Raquel over."

Sonny favored him. "As in your past love life?"

"Yeah—one woman in particular—Cassandra Tucker."

Sonny's brow furrowed. "Not much you can do to wipe the slate clean there, other than impress upon Raquel that it's the here and now that's important."

"I couldn't agree more," Keanu said, handing him the ball. "Guess I'll just have to keep working at it."

"You've always succeeded in anything you put your mind to. I'm sure that'll be the same thing in this case."

"Hope so. I'm really into her."

"I can see that." Sonny wiped perspiration from his brow. "So what is it about her that makes her so special?"

Keanu considered the question. "Apart from her obvious beauty, Raquel is so creative, smart, easy to talk to, and she has both feet on the ground. Other women have had this quality or that, but none have been able to put it all together in one incredible package like she has."

He didn't particularly like comparing one woman to another, as he respected them all in different ways. But in his mind there was no comparison between Raquel and the other women he'd been with. No woman before her had left the impression on him that Raquel had, both in bed and out. Whether that meant they had what it took to make this work for the long haul was something Keanu couldn't say at this point. But he would be damned if he didn't do everything in his power to convince Raquel that he was the man for her.

"Definitely sounds like a winner," Sonny said.

Keanu watched as his uncle missed the basket. "She is," he said. "And one hell of a hula dancer, too."

Sonny laughed. "A lady of many talents."

"Something like that." Not the least of which were her talents in the bedroom. Keanu once again had a vivid image of them together and felt a trifle aroused. "Most of all, I think Raquel has her act together and isn't one of those women who cares only about money instead of the real me. She is her own woman, with a very successful business and the guts to hold her own with other successful professionals like me. I could have used her during my playing days when my image took a hit or two."

"It's obvious to me that this woman makes you happier than any other I've seen—even if you've hit a rough patch at the moment. My guess is that she'll come around and realize that you're as sincere as sincere can be, and she'll grab on to a great man."

"Thanks, Unc." He tracked down the basketball and promptly shot an air ball. "I'm sure you're right."

"Wherever things go between the two of you, just promise me that you won't do anything rash, like elope and forget all about practical considerations, such as a prenuptial agreement."

Keanu grinned, knowing his uncle was looking out

for his best interests. "Don't worry, there won't be any elopement," he promised, preferring not to think too far ahead. Right now, he only wanted to get back on Raquel's good side as solid boyfriend material. Besides, he had a feeling that Raquel would want it done right if they were to get married. Meaning a formal Hawaiian wedding. All he wanted was for his first marriage to be his last one.

"Now I see why you ended your career," Sonny joked after he had pulled even in the game and put the pressure on Keanu. "Looks like you're losing your touch."

A chuckle escaped Keanu's mouth. "We'll see about that." He calmly lined up and sank a fifteen footer, which he could still do with his eyes closed. "Let's see if you can top that."

When Keanu's cell phone rang, he took it out of his pocket and saw that it was Raquel. He couldn't resist a smile, remembering when they had last laid eyes on one another.

"Hey," he said.

"Hi." She paused. "If you're not busy tonight, I was wondering if you'd like to come over for dinner."

Keanu didn't have to give it a second thought. "What time?"

"Seven?"

He punched in her address on the phone. "I'll see you then."

"Raquel?" Sonny gazed at him.

Keanu nodded, putting his phone away. "She invited me to dinner."

"Seems as though things are looking up."

"Yeah, I believe so," Keanu said.

"I'm betting she's a good cook too."

"I wouldn't expect otherwise."

"But can she play ball?" Sonny asked jokingly.

"I'm sure I'll find out one of these days." Keanu suspected that Raquel was good at basketball too and likely had many other hidden talents that he hoped to uncover. He shot the ball and watched it rattle the rim and roll off, giving Sonny the victory. Fortunately, Keanu was looking to triumph in other areas tonight.

Chapter 7

The moment Keanu set foot inside Raquel's house, his nose took in the scent of food mixed with a sweet fragrance coming from Raquel herself. She was stunning in a low-cut, dark green top and a white medallion print skirt, which showed off her shapely bare legs. Her pretty feet with crimson polished toenails were in thong sandals.

"Aloha," he said, and presented her with a single, long-stemmed red rose.

"Mahalo," she responded, beaming as she put the rose up to her nose. "And thanks for coming."

"My pleasure." Keanu smiled.

"Hungry?" Her full lips glistened.

"Yeah, I am," he answered. And not only for food. His desire to have her had only grown since he'd last seen her.

"Good. I put together something that I hope you'll like."

He gave her the once-over. "I see something right now that I definitely like."

"I'm serious," she pouted.

Keanu put his arms around her waist. "So am I.…" He attempted to kiss her lips, but she turned away.

"Don't," Raquel told him. "I was hoping we could talk."

"Let's talk later." He was still holding her. "I need you, baby."

"Are you sure it's me that you need?"

"I've never been more sure of anything in my life. This is real. I hope you feel it too.…"

"Maybe I do," she conceded. "But being in business together—"

Keanu put a finger to her lips. "It's just something we'll have to deal with. Don't let that stand in the way of what we can have.…"

His head tilted, and Keanu went for another kiss. This time Raquel did not turn her face, and she met his mouth with hers. They stayed that way for a while, enjoying the kiss.

"Sure you don't want to try the food first?" Raquel spoke into his mouth.

"Not when you're this damned close and so mesmerizing," Keanu responded huskily.

He kissed her again, and Raquel quickly slipped back under his spell. The rose slipped from her fingers, and they slid down to the plush carpeting. Keanu was sure she had a nice bed in there, but frankly he liked the idea of making love right there—not wanting to waste a moment to have her.

He caressed and kissed Raquel's silky-smooth, long legs. Then he removed her sandals and kissed her feet as she moaned. She liked that. He thought she would. He massaged them for a moment or two before moving back up, where he put his face underneath her skirt. Inhaling her mesmerizing scent, Keanu went to work using his teeth to push aside her underwear, then started to kiss and taste between Raquel's legs. Her core was seemingly made for his lips and tongue to enjoy. She was moaning from the stimulation he gave her. She became wet quickly, arousing him that much more. He loved giving a woman he cared for an orgasm the right way, so that later she could multiply that tenfold when he was inside.

"Oh, Keanu, you are too good," Raquel cried out raggedly.

"And you taste so delicious," he responded, licking her voraciously, "so I'd say we're enjoying ourselves equally."

He felt her grab his head and her body tremble as the moment of ecstasy hit her. Keanu smiled salaciously, wanting her now more than ever. When he came back up, he took a condom packet from his pocket. After pulling his slacks down to his ankles, he covered his full penis in a flash. He pushed up Raquel's skirt over her hips and removed her panties. He positioned himself between her spread legs before burrowing into her flesh and deep inside of her.

Raquel bent her knees and arched her back, meeting his potent thrusts halfway. Keanu braced himself with his strong arms while kissing her mouth ardently. They were turning her living room floor into their own private sex machine. He took in a long breath between kisses and continued to make love to Raquel, sliding deep inside the thick warmth of her walls, trembling slightly as the waves of pleasure rippled through his veins.

"Umm…ohh…ahh…" moaned Raquel as she tightened around him.

"Oh, yeah," Keanu said back to her, the lightning-quick action making him hot and extremely bothered.

He broke from her mouth and nibbled on her earlobes. She responded by grabbing his buttocks, widening her legs, and pushing his erection deeper into her with each plunge.

Their moist bodies quivered together as the frenetic pace and determination gripped them like a fever that wouldn't let up till satisfaction had been achieved. Keanu went back to sucking Raquel's mouth when his orgasm collided with hers and stars went off in his head while they exploded in sexual unison.

He fell onto the floor afterward, catching his breath and feeling as if he had definitely met his match when it came to sex. Raquel had made it easy for him to become hooked on their sexual compatibility. He didn't want to lose what they had found in each other.

"Wow," Raquel said, sighing, her breast pressed against his side. "Are you always this insatiable?"

"You make me want to make love all the time," he told her genuinely.

"Do you tell that to all the women you get in bed— or on the floor?"

Keanu gazed at her, realizing that she needed to be reassured as to where he stood in that regard. "No, I don't. I have never felt for anyone else the way I feel about you."

"Good answer." Raquel smiled. "I think the same is true in reverse. I'm not normally like this with someone I'm still getting to know."

He grinned. "It's good to know you're not like this with everyone."

She propped up on an elbow. "So I take it this means we are now officially involved, business aside?"

Keanu met her eyes. "Yeah, definitely."

"You really think it can work?"

"I'm positive it not only can, but will work, if we both give ourselves a chance to let it happen."

"I think so too." Raquel kissed his shoulder. "I'd better check on the food. Or have you lost your appetite?"

Never, where you're concerned. "No, just the opposite," Keanu declared. "I believe I've worked up a very good appetite."

Raquel honestly had not expected to have sex with Keanu. And certainly not practically the instant he stepped inside the door. Though she had been startled, she had adjusted to his overpowering desire for her before. It put her in the mood just as quickly and pushed her doubts about them to the back of her mind. Though she still had reservations, she knew she would no longer be able to resist finding out what sexual adventures awaited them and how they would play out against the backdrop of a professional relationship.

She watched from across her circular glass table as Keanu indulged himself in the meal of broiled sea scallops enveloped in bacon, Cajun lamb chops and hash brown potatoes, along with a bottle of Cabernet Sauvignon. She'd made upside-down apple pie for dessert.

"It's absolutely delicious," Keanu told her, his mouth stuffed with food.

Raquel smiled gratefully. "Looks like you're enjoying it."

"Let's see...talented businesswoman, sexy hula dancer, first-class swimmer, great lover and superb cook." Keanu sipped wine. "Have I left anything out?"

She laughed. "That's a good start. I'm sure you'll discover a few more things along the way."

A grin crossed his face. "Something to look forward to."

"I can say the same about you."

"So have you been working on some of the things we talked about for improving your image?" she asked, figuring this was a good time to bring it up since their minds weren't preoccupied with sexual thoughts.

"Yeah, as a matter of fact I have." He dabbed a napkin to a corner of his lips. "The nonprofit foundation is in progress even as we speak. I've also taken steps to do the basketball camp in a couple of weeks at my old high school."

A smile played on Raquel's lips as she set down her fork. "I see you've been busy."

"Hey, just doing what my adviser thinks would do wonders for my image."

"It should," she told him confidently. "And how about improving your wardrobe?"

Keanu gave a boyish grin. "Haven't gotten around to shopping for new clothes yet. Maybe you'd like to come with me to make sure I'm getting the right look?"

"I'd love to," Raquel said. "It's part of my job to keep on top of the latest styles."

"In that case, we'll pick outfits for me together, and

the outside world will get to see me in an entirely different light."

"Sounds nice." She eyed him, fresh from the memory of their sex. "Of course, I'm getting quite comfortable seeing you in little to no clothes at all. But that's just me."

He laughed. "Ditto."

Raquel warmed at the thought of their lovemaking. He'd made it all seem so totally natural. And the comfort she now felt sitting at her dinner table with him was too real and precious to ruin with thoughts of his past.

She took her mind away from their personal relationship, wanting to stick with the business relationship for the moment.

"As far as a great image booster goes, one thing you might want to consider at some point is participating in the Basketball Without Borders program," she told Keanu. It was an annual basketball summer camp for young people held in different parts of the world with a mission to promote health, education, friendship, leadership and good sportsmanship. The BWB sponsors included the NBA and the International Basketball Federation.

"I'd be happy to get involved with the BWB," he responded enthusiastically. "I thought about it during my playing days in the NBA, but was always too committed with other things during the off season."

Raquel grinned. "Wonderful. I'm sure the program could use someone like you to help those of lesser means with not only basketball skills, but also things such as the power in reading, HIV and life skills."

"I'll give the commissioner a call and talk about it," he said.

"If you find yourself in Africa or Asia for the Basketball Without Borders camp, maybe I can accompany you and be of some assistance," she said, realizing it would be good for her résumé as well as a means to spend more time with him in a very different environment.

"You'd really do that?" Keanu asked.

She nodded. "I think it would be fun." *Especially with you to keep me company and comfy at night.*

He smiled seductively as though reading her thoughts. "Yeah, I agree. We'll see if we can make it happen."

That was good enough, as far as Raquel was concerned. She was happy that Keanu was so quick to implement her ideas to create a more positive image for himself. Maybe much of what had been said about him was way off base after all. Or had he simply grown up quickly and finally realized that it was time to become more serious if he wanted to leave a legacy to be proud of?

If so, she assumed that included being a one-woman man who was willing to build a real relationship. Raquel took solace in that thought, hoping that she may have at last met someone who wanted the same things she did out of life and love. And she was willing to step out on a limb to make it happen.

A few days later, Raquel went with Lauren to the Waikiki Beach Walk, a well-developed stretch of Waikiki with an array of shops, restaurants, entertainment and cultural programs. They stopped at a bistro called Coffee Time.

"Sounds like you and Keanu have made a real splash,

if you'll pardon the pun," Lauren said over her espresso macchiato.

"You could say that," Raquel responded, grinning while sipping a green tea latte. They had talked earlier about how the swimming at Keanu's house didn't go very far, but was more than made up for in other ways.

"Why am I not surprised?" Lauren said. "You two really do seem to be a good match—even if it means Keanu's number one fan has to take a backseat to his new lady."

Raquel smiled softly. "You'll never have to take a backseat to my relationship with Keanu," she assured her. "I'm sure his fans will always be an important part of his life."

Lauren tasted her drink. "Doesn't hurt my cause any that he happens to be dating my best friend."

Raquel chuckled. "Not at all."

"So much for business and pleasure not mixing."

"They're *still* separate in our relationship," Raquel pointed out. "I'll continue to work with Keanu as a client who just happens to be very affectionate and hot."

"And just how *hot* is he in bed?" Lauren asked. "I can only imagine what athleticism he's displayed."

Raquel nearly laughed out loud, but didn't want to attract attention. "Red hot," she had to admit, and thought of Keanu in action, touching, tasting, kissing and making love to her tirelessly. "And yes, there has been a bit of athleticism there, both ways."

Lauren laughed. "Join the club, girlfriend. Victor's pretty hot to trot in that department, too."

"Looks like we both lucked out."

"Seems like it." Lauren sipped her macchiato.

"I guess anything's possible."

"I guess it is." Lauren eyed her. "Now that you've got the ins with Keanu, maybe you can get him to invite your girlfriend over to that palace he lives in. I've been dying to see it."

Raquel smiled. "I'll see what I can do. But since Victor's his friend, you could probably get in the front door that way too."

"Maybe, but you know how guys are with their egos. If I seem to be too ga-ga over Keanu, even in a non-sexual context, Victor might get bent out of shape."

"I see your point," Raquel said, lifting her drink. "Men can be so insecure." She knew the same applied to women. She still wasn't too comfortable with Keanu's past womanizing, and had a few doubts that he was truly past that. But she had decided to suppress her fears and, for once, just let herself be swept away. "No problem. I'm sure I can arrange for Keanu to give you a personal tour of his digs."

"Aloha au ia 'oe!" Lauren beamed.

"I love you too," Raquel assured her.

Chapter 8

Raquel was talking on the phone when Keanu stepped into her office to pick her up for a shopping spree at the nearby Aloha Tower Marketplace. She smiled upon seeing his handsome face, and gestured for him to come in farther while she wrapped up things with another client.

"Hi there," she told Keanu as he walked over to her.

"Aloha," he said, bending over and kissing her on the mouth.

She picked up the unfamiliar scent of his cologne. "That smells good. What is it?"

He grinned proudly. "Actually, it's Keanu, my own brand."

"Look at you," she teased. "Not everyone can be so fortunate to have their own fragrance line."

"There's a female version called Keanune that's

doing better than the male version, not too surprisingly."

Her lashes fluttered. Was he trying to make her jealous with thoughts of other women lusting after him through his scent?

"That's nice. So when do I get a bottle from my man?"

Keanu's chin dimple deepened. "I just happen to have one in my car for you."

She flushed. "That's so sweet."

"Not half as sweet as the perfume will smell on your sexy body, baby."

Raquel felt aroused at the thought of him smelling her from head to toe. "We'll see about that."

"Are you ready to go?" he asked.

"Yes." She couldn't wait to help outfit him with a new wardrobe that would be more appropriate for a successful businessman. Not that he looked anything but fine in his taupe shirt with stripes and straight-leg dark jeans.

During the drive Keanu told her about his meeting with his financial adviser.

"We discussed some initial funding for my nonprofit foundation, as well as creating an endowment fund for my alma mater."

"Very good," Raquel said, particularly impressed that he'd taken the initiative to set up an endowment fund at the University of Hawaii. "Looks like you've been busy."

"All part of the image building you got me started on," Keanu said from behind the wheel.

"You've certainly taken some key steps in that

regard. Before long no one will even remember all the negative stuff the press had to say about you."

He chuckled. "Some people have long memories. But that's their problem. I'm happy where I am right now." His hand fell across her lap. "And who I'm with."

"That goes for me, too," she told him, caressing his long fingers. She was beginning to believe that he truly was changing for the better right before her very eyes.

They stopped in front of the Marketplace's main entrance and a valet attendant parked the car. Inside, Raquel and Keanu were holding hands and headed toward a boutique specializing in men's high-end clothes when they were approached by a group of teenagers.

"Aren't you Keanu Bailey?" said a tall, almond-skinned boy.

Keanu smiled. "Yes."

"Can I get your autograph?"

"Me too," said a pretty girl with Senegalese twists.

"Sure," Keanu said, glancing at Raquel, who offered a supportive smile.

She watched as he signed pieces of paper and even one person's shirt. Raquel figured it was a clear indication that Keanu was becoming more open to giving back to his fans and expecting nothing in return but gratitude. It also told her that as long as he remained popular, Keanu would perhaps always be called upon as the basketball star, even when he was just trying to be Keanu her boyfriend. This was something she would simply have to learn to live with.

In the store, Keanu tried on clothes with Raquel giving her expert opinion on the latest trends and on how to present a professional image. He wound up buying several expensive designer single- and double-breasted suits, a tweed sport coat, some khaki shirts and fashion T-shirts and a pair of crocodile shoes and suede slippers. As she wanted this to be all about him, Raquel resisted the urge to add to her own wardrobe, promising to come back another time.

For dinner, they ordered Chinese food, and fed each other at Raquel's place. They made love in her bed, taking their time in exploring one another from head to toe, before cuddling for some rest after the sexual workout.

The chime of his cell phone woke Keanu up. Raquel's leg and arm were draped across him, and the scent of their sexual activity was pleasantly thick in the air. He almost hated to break up this serenity.

This had better be something good, he thought.

He slid from beneath her and used an outstretched arm to reach his jeans and grab his iPhone from the pocket. The caller ID showed it was a friend of his from the NBA, Derek Gilmore. They played with each other at Detroit and hung out together before Derek was traded to Phoenix, then cut at the end of the season. As far as Keanu knew, no one had picked him up.

"Guess where I'm calling from."

"You're in Honolulu?" Keanu's brow rose.

"Damned near," Derek said. "I'm chillin' on a Hawaiian singles cruise."

"Getting into trouble at sea, huh?" Keanu joked, eyeing Raquel's bare buttocks.

"Yeah, maybe a little." Derek laughed. "I figured since I seem to have a lot of unwanted time on my hands these days, I might as well use it to have a little fun."

"Nothing wrong with that."

"Figured you could relate," Derek said.

Keanu gave an uncomfortable chuckle. He was happy to have left the NBA on his own terms.

"So you're coming here?" Keanu asked.

"Matter of fact, I am," answered Derek. "We'll be docking in your hometown for a few hours tomorrow night. Maybe we can get together for a drink and some laughs. Talk about old times."

"Sounds good to me," Keanu said.

After hanging up, Keanu faced Raquel, kissing her on the lips.

"Who's coming to visit?" she asked.

Keanu told her, thinking she might not be familiar with Derek as he wasn't exactly a marquee player.

"I've heard of Derek Gilmore," Raquel insisted.

"He's on a cruise ship that's headed our way." Keanu played with her loose hair. "I told him we could get together around eight tomorrow at Antonio's nightclub."

"We?" She batted her eyes. "You sure you don't want it to be a boys' night out?"

He grinned. "I'm not into that these days, remember? Besides, I want to show off my new lady."

She smiled. "In that case, I'd be honored to tag along and meet your friend."

"Fortunately, that's tomorrow. Tonight is still all ours."

She wet her lips. "Haven't you had enough for one night?"

"Have you?" He tossed the question back.

"Only one way to find out," she cooed, sliding her leg down his and back up again.

As his erection quickly grew, Keanu had little doubt that neither of them were ready to call it a night.

Raquel took one look at the man inside the club and realized she needed to look up farther. She guessed he was six-eight, maybe taller, dwarfing her even in high-heeled pumps. He was also bald and heavier than he'd looked when she had last seen him on a televised game.

Keanu introduced them and Derek took her hand and kissed the back of it.

"A-lo-ha," he said. "Keanu didn't tell me he had someone so lovely in his backyard."

"Mahalo," Raquel responded, not particularly impressed with his obviously practiced line. She wondered how many ladies on the cruise had fallen for it, or him.

"Maybe I need to relocate to Honolulu where all the beautiful women apparently live," Derek declared.

"I think there's more than a few to be found on the mainland," she told him, smelling the alcohol on his breath.

"And some of them are actually available," Keanu said with a territorial tone of voice.

Derek grinned crookedly. "Yeah, I heard that."

Raquel was glad to see that Keanu was setting some ground rules, just in case Derek thought she was just another pretty face to Keanu.

"Why don't we find somewhere to sit?" suggested Keanu.

They sat and ordered cocktails.

"Heard from any of the teams about possible interest?" Keanu asked Derek.

He furrowed his brow. "My agent talked to Dallas and Sacramento. So far that's all it is—talk."

"I'm sure some playoff-bound team looking for a push will give you a ring."

"One can only hope," muttered Derek.

"There's always Europe and China," Keanu said. "I have friends playing in both places."

"Thanks, but I think I'd rather stick to American soil."

The drinks came and Keanu paid for them.

Raquel noticed that Derek couldn't seem to take his eyes off her. "So how are you enjoying the cruise so far?" she asked, if only to put his mind elsewhere.

He grinned. "It's been a lot of fun, but I'm only halfway through. Meaning there's still time to get lucky—"

Her face flushed at the obvious sexual reference. She turned to Keanu, preferring that he take over the conversation.

"How's your brother doing?" Keanu adeptly changed the subject, adding for Raquel, "He's a top NBA point guard prospect, playing for Oregon State University."

"Ricky's just waiting his turn," Derek said. "Trying to keep doing his thing without getting hurt."

"Cool." Keanu gazed at Raquel, offering a comforting smile.

She returned it, happy to be in his company, even if she could do without Derek and his over-the-top style.

An older couple, wearing leis, walked up to their table. "Are you Keanu Bailey?" the man asked, looking at him.

Keanu nodded. "Yeah."

"My wife and I are from Detroit and are big fans of yours."

Keanu's lips curved into a smile. "Good to hear. Aloha to you both."

"Aloha," the two said in unison.

"Here all the way from the Motor City, huh?" Keanu asked.

"We've always wanted to visit Hawaii," the woman said, patting her gray bob. "Seeing you here is definitely the highlight of the trip."

"Do you mind taking a picture with us in front of the club?" her husband asked Keanu.

"Uh, sure, I'd be happy to," he said.

After Keanu and his fans stepped away, Raquel found Derek's massive hand atop hers. She quickly yanked hers away.

"So how long have you and Keanu been together?" he asked.

"Long enough," she snorted.

"Keanu's a stand-up guy and all, but you can do much better."

Raquel frowned. "Excuse me?"

Derek put his hand on hers again, clutching her wrist. "I'm just saying, if you ever get tired of him and want to give a real man a try, I'm available."

"Not interested." She tried wriggling her hand free, but his grip was too tight. "I suggest you let go of my hand—now!"

"A feisty one," he said. "Just the type I like. We can have a lot of fun together."

"What's the hell's going on here?" boomed the voice of Keanu.

Derek immediately released Raquel's hand, a sheepish grin on his face. "We were just talking."

Keanu looked at Raquel. "Everything all right?"

She was furious, but didn't want to make a scene at the club or cause a confrontation between him and Keanu.

"Everything's fine," she said tersely.

Keanu didn't seem convinced, peering at Derek. "Did you step out of line with my girl, man?"

"Not at all," he responded innocently. "Since when did you get so possessive over a chick?"

"When some asshole was hitting on her behind my back," Keanu said hotly.

"Just your imagination. Everything's cool between her and me," Derek said. "Isn't that right?"

Raquel had a mind to tell him exactly what she thought. But what good would that do? When she was trying to get Keanu to control his temper, the last thing she needed was to incite violence from him. It would be a huge step backward in his image rebuilding. Not to mention risky if Keanu got hurt in a fight with Derek, who was much bigger.

"He didn't do anything," she said quietly.

"See, I told you." Derek's face brightened.

Keanu sighed. "Okay."

"So how about another round of drinks?" Derek asked, clearly happy to put the whole thing behind him.

"I think I'd like to go now," Raquel said, peering at Keanu.

He gave her a look of surprise. "Already?"

"Yes, I'm not feeling very well," she lied.

Keanu pursed his lips. "Then we'll go."

Raquel gave Derek a scathing look and he wisely remained mute.

During the drive home, Keanu asked tersely, "You want to tell me what happened at the club?"

"Nothing."

"You're sure about that?" he pressed.

"I'm just tired," she said.

"Tired or not feeling well?"

"Both." Her nostrils flared. "Why don't we just leave it at that, okay?"

Keanu's head fell back. "If you say so."

They hardly spoke for the rest of the drive as Raquel wrestled with her thoughts. She loved that Keanu was a retired and still popular ballplayer with a lot to offer a woman. But should that include having to put up with his oversexed and inebriated athlete pals disrespecting her? Was this what she was in for if they remained a couple over the long haul?

Raquel sent Keanu home, deciding she'd rather sleep alone tonight, even if she longed for his touch, scent and physical comfort.

The following day, Keanu was still uneasy about what had gone down between Raquel and Derek at the club. Both had acted weirdly when he got back to the table and afterward. The fact that Raquel had wanted to go home, but couldn't seem to make up her mind why, told him something wasn't right.

As he shot some hoops, Keanu considered his days of partying hard with Derek, as well as his friend's well-deserved reputation for chasing women. At last count, Derek had gotten at least three women pregnant, marrying one that ended in divorce quickly. Could he have brazenly tried to put the moves on Raquel?

Feeling he needed some answers, Keanu started to call Raquel but then decided a face-to-face meeting was better. He showed up at her place and was glad to see she was there.

"Why didn't you call first?" she asked, her hand on the hip of her terry bathrobe.

"Some things are better said in person," he said. "So can I come in?"

Raquel rolled her eyes and stepped aside so Keanu could come in. "I really need to get ready for work—"

"What the hell happened last night between you and Derek?" Keanu rounded on her.

"I already told you, it was nothing," she said, averting her gaze.

"So why do I feel I'm missing something here?"

"Maybe because you're letting your imagination run rampant for no reason," she replied.

Keanu knew that at times he had an overactive imagination, but this wasn't one of those times. Why was she lying to him? Why would she try to protect Derek if he did something out of line?

He took out his phone. "If you want, I'll phone Derek right now, put him on the speaker and make him tell me why we left the club so abruptly."

Raquel sighed. "All right… Your friend *completely* disrespected me…and you."

Keanu's eyes narrowed. "How?"

"He made a pass at me, grabbing my hand, and didn't seem to want to take no for an answer. Till you showed up."

"That bastard," said Keanu. "Why didn't you tell me last night?"

"I didn't want to make a big deal out of it," Raquel said softly.

"It is a *very* big deal when some jerk I thought was

my friend comes on to my girlfriend." Keanu shouldn't have been too surprised, given the type of person he knew Derek to be. But he had still crossed the line and it was inexcusable.

"Just let it go," Raquel implored.

"Like you did when we left the club because you were tired and not feeling well?" he asked sarcastically.

"I thought it was best at the time," she explained. "I didn't want any trouble between you and him. There was no need to sink to his level, especially when you're trying to stay even-tempered as part of your image transformation."

Keanu sucked in a deep breath. He may not have been happy that she kept this from him, but he understood her rationale. As his image consultant and girlfriend, she was trying to look out for his best interests. Damn Derek for being such a jerk. Why make a play for Raquel with so many other single women out there looking for love or sex?

He'd be sure to give Derek a call later and let him know exactly what he thought of his appalling behavior.

Keanu walked over and put his arms around Raquel, feeling the warmth radiating from her body. "I'm sorry for snapping at you," he told her sincerely. "I appreciate that you took the high road."

"It wasn't easy," she said. "I felt like slapping Derek, but given his size, thought better of it."

Keanu couldn't argue with her logic there. It probably would have been foolish as well for him to come to blows with Derek, even if he deserved to be taught a lesson. Keanu had no desire to make more negative headlines and, in the process, take a step backward in his professional and personal relationship with Raquel.

"You did the right thing," he said, kissing the top of her head.

She pulled back, gazing up at him. "You really believe that?"

"Yes." He met her eyes. "At least he's gone now and can wreak havoc somewhere else."

Raquel's brow creased. "Please tell me that's not what I have to look forward to with all your friends."

Keanu moved his head obliquely. "It isn't," he said. "Athletes often get a bad rap, though in some cases it's totally justified. But most will not go after another guy's woman and have the gall to think they'll get away with it."

She sighed. "Good to know, because dodging men with wandering eyes and hands is not the way I envision living my life."

"I hear you," Keanu said. At the same time, Keanu knew that with Raquel's ravishing beauty and the way she carried herself, men would always be attracted to her and try to make a move on her. But jealousy had already done enough damage to their still-fresh relationship, and he knew they would both have to learn to deal with it.

"In that case, I think I'd better get dressed," Raquel said.

"I'd much rather see you get undressed," Keanu said seductively.

She batted her eyes at him. "I'll just bet you would."

He held her cheeks and gave her a solid kiss on the lips. "You sure you can't be a tiny bit late for work?"

Raquel licked her lips. "That's not fair, getting me worked up like that."

"I never play fair where it concerns desire," Keanu said and kissed her again. He unfastened her robe and saw that she had nothing beneath other than her bare butterscotch-brown skin. Her shapely body automatically turned him on every time he laid eyes on it.

"Hmm…" murmured Raquel as Keanu caressed her nipples. "Maybe I can be just a little late, as long as you make it worth my while."

He grinned lasciviously, sliding a hand between her legs. "Consider it done."

Taking her into his arms, Keanu carried her into the bedroom where they made each second count. After they climaxed simultaneously with Raquel on top riding Keanu like a thoroughbred, he held on to her buttocks and relished the intense sensations till the experience had completed its hold on their bodies.

Keanu watched from the bed as Raquel got dressed, admiring her every curve.

"If you want to stay in bed all day, be my guest," she teased him.

"I'll take you up on that when we can spend all day in bed together."

She grinned. "You really are voracious!"

"Guilty as charged," he said. "I think you have something—actually a lot—to do with that."

"I'd better," she said over her shoulder. "By the way, do you have any plans for Thanksgiving?"

Keanu thought about it. "No, not really. My uncle and his wife are headed to the Big Island to spend the weekend with her brother and family."

"My mom said I could invite a guest to Thanksgiving dinner at her man friend's house. I was hoping you'd be interested."

"Count me in," he said. "I was wondering when you'd finally get around to introducing me to your mother."

"I wanted to give us time to get to know each other first," Raquel said, stepping into her clogs.

He stood up and sauntered over to her, getting in a bear hug from behind. "I'd say we've gotten to know each other pretty damned well by now."

"Other than in bed," she hummed, sliding from his grasp.

"That too." Keanu grabbed his pants off the floor. "I'm looking forward to meeting your mother and her man."

"She might talk your head off," Raquel warned.

He grinned. "Good. Maybe I can pick up a few other tidbits about you along the way."

She laughed. "You think so?"

"One can only try," Keanu said lightly. He wanted to know as much as possible about the woman who had suddenly become a very big part of his life, and he hoped an even bigger part of his future.

Chapter 9

Raquel was a trifle nervous about introducing her mother to Keanu. The fact that he was her boyfriend and a millionaire ex-basketball player—who also happened to be very good-looking and very into her—made Raquel fear that her mother might believe they were practically already engaged, with children right around the corner. The truth was, their relationship was still growing and neither was talking about love or marriage just yet. Not that she wasn't hoping this was in the cards for her and Keanu. But another part of her wondered if she could handle being with someone still caught up in the spotlight. Including ex-NBA friends who thought they were entitled to act like first-class jerks.

Those thoughts were tucked away in the back of Raquel's mind as she and Keanu arrived at the house of her mother's boyfriend on Thanksgiving. Sean Hawthorne, whom her mother had met at church, was a widower and retired pilot. Even if something inside of Raquel wanted Davetta to cling to her father's memory, overall she wanted her mother to move on and find happiness. She apparently had with Sean.

Now it was Raquel's turn to do the same. So far so good with Keanu. He was holding her hand as they walked up to the door of a beautiful ranch home in Makiki Heights, located on a slope above Honolulu. She looked up at Keanu, who looked dashing in one of his new suits, a navy stripe sharkskin suit. Using her pinky, she wiped lipstick from his mouth where they had just kissed.

"That's better," she whispered to him. "You can take more off my lips later."

"Count on it," he said, with a sexy smile.

The door opened and Raquel saw Sean standing there. He was in his sixties and about as tall as Keanu, but a bit thinner with a horseshoe-shaped white hairline. He had a cream-colored suit on with shoes that matched.

"Hey, Sean," Raquel said sweetly.

"Aloha, Raquel." He gave her a kiss on the cheek and turned to Keanu. "No introductions are needed here. I'd recognize your face anywhere." He laughed, putting out his hand. "Nice to meet you, Keanu."

"You too," he said, giving Sean a toothy smile.

"Come on in, both of you."

Raquel had barely gotten through the door when she heard her mother's voice. "I was hoping you didn't lose your way."

"Not with your detailed directions." Though this

was her first time visiting the house, Raquel knew the area well enough, as Lauren lived nearby. She gave her mother a hug.

Davetta, wearing a tropical hibiscus spaghetti-strap dress, marched past her and approached Keanu. "I'm Raquel's mom. Nice to finally meet you."

"The feeling is mutual," he told her.

"Can I give you a hug?" she asked.

"Of course." Keanu leaned down and she put her arms around his neck. He kissed her cheek.

"Mahalo," Davetta said. "You know, I thought you had at least one good year left in you."

Keanu laughed. "Probably." He put his arm around Raquel. "But leaving when I did gave me the chance to meet your lovely daughter. Can't fault me for that, can you?"

"Not at all," she assured him. "I can see we'll get along just fine."

"Yes, I think we will," he said.

Raquel smiled, thinking that things had gotten off to a good start. She only hoped that her mother didn't get too comfortable with Keanu and begin talking about stuff he may not be ready to get into. Such as his intentions with her.

"I watched you in the last All Star game," Sean commented to Keanu as they sat in the dining room at a glass-top table. "I thought you outplayed LeBron and Durant and should've at least been co-MVP."

Keanu grinned as he sliced into one of the thick pieces of turkey on his plate that was crowded by cornbread dressing, sweet potatoes and broccoli. "Much of it has nothing to do with how well you play," he explained, "so much as where you're playing and who's most popular at the time. Being with the Pistons, though a solid team, didn't give me the same spotlight as when I was in L.A."

"You'll always be number one on the islands," Davetta said, smiling at him. "Right alongside Obama."

"Well, it's always nice to share the stage with Obama," he told her and winked at Raquel, who sat beside him. She looked amazing in a one-shoulder purple-knit dress. This seemed like the perfect time to see what he could discover about her from the right source. "What was Raquel like as a child?" he asked Davetta.

Raquel put her hands to her face in embarrassment. "You don't want to go there."

"I'm afraid I do."

"She was spoiled rotten as an only child," Davetta said. "And also a tomboy. She could run, swim and play basketball with the best of them. I used to wonder if she'd ever come to terms with being a girl and someday a lady."

Keanu laughed, finding it hard to imagine Raquel being anything but a lady. He looked at her. "You didn't tell me you played ball."

"You never asked," she responded, fluttering her lashes.

"She probably also didn't tell you that she speaks three languages and graduated at the top of her class," Davetta said.

"No kidding?" Keanu turned to Raquel with a cocked brow. She clearly had even more going on than he realized, making her all the more impressive as a woman.

"Will you cut it out, Mom?" she pressed. "Keanu has probably already had an earful about how great I am."

He laughed. "I'm glad to know all your little secrets," he told her.

Her eyes widened. "Oh really…?"

"Yeah. It helps round things out and tells me just what a great catch you are."

Raquel blushed. "I think you know the feeling's mutual."

"Obviously what we have here are two very talented individuals who happened to find each other," remarked Sean over his wineglass. "Kind of like me and Davetta."

"That's right," she said.

"I'll drink to that," Keanu said with a grin and proceeded to lift his glass of wine.

"Tell us about your family, Keanu," Davetta said, dabbing the corners of her mouth with a cloth napkin.

"Okay…" He spoke of the tragedy of his parents' death and how his Uncle Sonny had taken him in, raising him like his own son, and added how Ashley had come into the picture and become a member of the family. "As a matter of fact," Keanu said as the thought entered his head, "I'd like to invite everyone to my house for Christmas dinner—if you don't have other plans. It would be great for our families to get together. Don't you think, Raquel?"

Her eyes twinkled. "Yes, that would be nice, if it's what you really want."

"It is," he assured her. "What better way to spend Christmas than with family?"

"You're right," she said and turned to her mother.

"That's very kind of you," Davetta said. "Sean and

I would love to visit with your family for a Christmas Day meal. I'd even be happy to help cook."

Keanu smiled. "Thanks, but Uncle Sonny is the cook in our family and loves to do his own thing with maybe just a little help from Ashley."

"Now that you're retired from the NBA," began Davetta, setting her fork down, "are you looking to settle down and have a family of your own?"

Raquel frowned. "Mom, please—"

"What?" She looked at her with a creased brow. "It's an honest question."

"Your mother has a good point," said Keanu. He met Davetta's steadfast stare. "Yes, as a matter of fact. I'm at the stage of my life where I'm ready to settle down."

"Ready to leave the playboy lifestyle behind you, aye?" Sean asked with amusement.

"Yeah, I think I am," Keanu responded. He knew that his reputation as a ladies' man preceded him, whether he liked it or not, but he hoped that Raquel believed that his interest in her was more than just a passing fancy. His eyes shifted to her. He could picture her as a wife and mother. Was that in her plans? Or did she see herself as the consummate businesswoman and lover, with no time for kids and a husband?

"I hope you weren't too overwhelmed by my mother putting you on the spot with some of her questions," Raquel said to Keanu in the car. "And it looks like Sean has picked up some of her traits."

Keanu chuckled as he leaned back in the passenger seat. "Not at all. It works both ways with the questions. I came away with more knowledge about you and they got a little something in return."

"Hmm…" Raquel thought about her mother spilling the beans about her childhood and achievements. She supposed it was a good thing for Keanu to know more about who she was, even if she had learned to take her accomplishments in stride. Probably as he had with his skills.

"So what languages do you speak?" he asked as though reading her thoughts.

"English, Hawaiian and French," she told him.

"Cool. I'm right with you on the first two. Maybe one of these days you can give me some French lessons."

She flashed him a smile. "Anytime."

"And I can probably teach you a few things on the basketball court," he said.

"You think?" Raquel laughed.

"Or maybe it's the other way around, if you've still got some of that tomboy in you," Keanu said.

"I think it comes out every now and then," she told him, thinking of the gymnastics they did sometimes when having sex.

He grinned. "Yeah, I agree."

"So where to?" She would welcome some relaxation after the meal. Maybe a walk on the beach, hand in hand.

"Let's go back to my place," he suggested. "We can check out that secluded beach and see what the ocean is up to."

Raquel beamed. "That sounds wonderful."

She wondered just how serious Keanu was about settling down. Did he even truly know what it meant to settle down with one woman and build a family together? Or was it more of a fantasy for someone who, by most accounts, had never stuck very long with one woman?

Raquel hoped that she had managed to single-hand-edly hook the former NBA star into reforming his past ways and getting serious about a possible future to-gether. She loved the thought of being Mrs. Keanu Bailey someday, even if the reality still seemed far off.

On a Saturday in the first week of December, Keanu held his first basketball camp for underprivileged chil-dren, some of whom lived in his old neighborhood. He'd recruited Victor to help out, along with a couple of volunteer students from his alma mater. The kids were given free Keanu Bailey–brand gym shoes, then put through a few standard basketball drills, and given tips on shooting free throws and jump shots.

"Looks like you've got them feeling like they're on top of the world," Victor remarked, a whistle around his neck.

"Yeah." Keanu looked at the kids jumping and bouncing around, just the way he used to. He tossed a ball to one of them. "Who knows which ones may turn out to be the next Oscar Robertson, Carmelo Anthony or Keanu Bailey."

"The road has to start somewhere," agreed Victor. "Seems like someone else is on top of the world these days too...."

Keanu arched a brow. "Who...me?"

"I'm not looking at anyone else right now."

Keanu grinned. "Guess I am feeling pretty good these days." He picked up an errant ball and bounced it.

"Something tells me it has to do with a certain

lady named Raquel," Victor said, taking the ball from Keanu.

"By *something,* I take it you mean Lauren told you," Keanu said.

"Yeah, she keeps me up to speed." Victor shot the ball off the backboard, watching it fall into the basket.

Keanu scratched his chin. "I won't deny it. Raquel's become very special to me. We're just clicking on all fronts." It amazed him, considering the past women in his life who were rarely able to hold his attention for very long. But with Raquel, he only wanted to get closer, not back away.

Victor's eyelids lowered. "So where do you see things going between you two?"

"As far as they can," Keanu said, taking the ball from him.

"Wow." Victor laughed. "You've got a serious case of it, don't you?"

"I guess I do," he said, tossing up a hook shot that went in. He watched as the kids scrambled for the ball. There was no denying what Keanu was beginning to feel in his heart. If he and Raquel were on the same wavelength, then there were no mountains they couldn't climb in their relationship.

"I'm happy for you, man," Victor told him. "About time you hooked up with someone who really does it for you."

Keanu grinned. "I could say the same thing about you. The way I hear it, you and Lauren are hot to trot for each other."

"Yeah, we're tight," said Victor. "We'll see how things go."

"That's about all you can do," Keanu agreed thoughtfully. He could only hope that the future held the type of life he could imagine with Raquel.

Victor gazed toward the door. "Well, look who's here…"

Keanu turned and saw Raquel approaching. He headed toward her, smiling all the while. "I didn't expect to see you."

"I wanted to surprise you," she told him. "Thought you might be able to use an extra hand with the kids."

He sized her up. She wore an orange scoop-neck tank top, tight cropped jeans and wedge sneakers. Her hair was pulled into a ponytail.

"Any opportunity to spend some time with you is fine by me," he said, planting a kiss on her sweet lips.

She blushed. "The feeling's mutual."

"Not to mention, it will give me the chance to see what you can do on the court."

Raquel batted her lashes. "I thought this was all about the kids?"

"It is, as you can see." Keanu looked around at the crowd that had shown up for the free basketball camp. "That won't let you off the hook, though." He tracked down a ball. "Let's see what you've got, woman."

She laughed. "If you insist. Just don't take it personally if I show you a thing or two."

His head fell back with laughter. "I think I'll take it very personally," he said. He couldn't wait to watch every twist and turn of that hot body on the court.

Chapter 10

In spite of the bumpy ride from Oahu to Kauai, Raquel was glad to have an overnight respite from life in Honolulu to dance with Kym and Peter Ogtong. The fact that Keanu had accompanied them made it all the more exciting and ensured that they could make a little romantic escape out of it. The gig would take place at a posh hotel in the town of Kapa'a on the island's Coconut Coast, overlooked by the Nounou Mountain known as the "Sleeping Giant."

Inside the dressing room, Raquel put on her costume, which was a skimpy bikini top and a *pa'u* skirt made of *lauhala,* or dried leaves from a hala tree. She placed leis made from fragrant plants around her head and neck, and decorative *kupe'e* encircled her wrists and ankles. Feeling she was all set for the show, she stepped out to an area where Keanu was allowed to wait.

"What do you think?" she asked, doing a 360-degree turn to model the costume.

"You look marvelous," he responded, grinning broadly. "Very traditional, but with a generous dose of sexiness."

Raquel laughed, knowing that the amount of skin showing could be considered just a bit risqué. "Well, I hope you like the show. It's not my normal thing, but after practicing with Kym and Peter, I think I can get through the performance without falling flat on my face or getting burned." She meant that last part literally, as Peter's fire dancing required lots of twirls and other movement, bringing the fire uncomfortably close to her and Kym. However, Kym had assured her that Peter had never had an accident to date. Raquel wanted to keep it that way, as she wasn't sure how Keanu would feel if her luscious hair got singed. Or worse.

"No doubt I'll love watching you do your thing with Peter and Kym," Keanu told her. "This naughty side of you is much more compelling than the business-woman."

"Oh, you think so?" she asked teasingly.

"Definitely."

She ran a hand down the side of his square jaw and whispered, "Later I'll show you just how naughty I can be."

He grinned. "Now that's a performance I can't wait to see."

"I'll bet." Raquel tiptoed on her bare feet and kissed him deeply, giving him a taste of things to come. But first she had some dancing to do.

She joined Kym and Peter for some final rehearsing.

"You're such a natural at this, Raquel," Peter told her

as the three of them danced in rhythm. He was a hulking Filipino man with long jet-black hair pulled into a ponytail. He wore only a *malo,* or loincloth, and was adorned with lei and *kupe'e* around his head, neck and wrists.

"I think it's more like practice makes perfect," she said, trying hard to keep up with him.

"We do make a pretty good trio," chirped Kym, whose colorful costume and accessories matched Raquel's.

"Better hold that thought till after the show," Raquel warned.

"You'll do just fine." Peter put a huge arm around her shoulders. "If not, Keanu and I may have to leave you behind in Kauai. But I also heard you're an excellent swimmer so you shouldn't have any problem getting back to Honolulu."

She laughed and elbowed him lightly in the ribs. "I think I'll ace the performance and everyone will leave happy."

"Now you're talking," he said, grinning.

"So let's give them a dance act to remember," Kym said.

Raquel sucked in a breath. "Ready when you are."

When they stepped onto the stage, she left her butterflies behind, determined to make not only Kym and Peter proud, but also Keanu, who was sitting in a front-row seat with his undivided attention on her.

Keanu sipped on a mojito while sitting back and enjoying the performance. Beneath a starlit sky, Polynesian drummers thumped away to the music of Hawaii,

Tahiti and Samoa. Raquel and Kym danced while Peter weaved in and out of them with his fire-knife dancing.

Raquel flashed a thousand-watt smile at Keanu as she sashayed across the stage close to him. She captivated Keanu as she moved her body gracefully and seductively, shaking her hips, swaying her arms and showing athleticism with her strong legs and nimble feet. He loved how erotic and breathtaking she was as a hula dancer, and it was clear that she was right at home before an audience.

Keanu had no problem with his lady capturing the imagination of other men when she danced. After all, she only shared her body with him. He would never become possessive like some men he knew, which only showed weakness and insecurity. Having been on the other end of popularity and sexual appeal, he understood that it came with the territory when one was good-looking, talented and sexy.

I've got everything I could want in a woman with Raquel. She makes me feel complete.

He focused back on her exotic and seemingly tireless dancing, exchanging smiles with her as he thought: *I must be the luckiest man on the islands, as Raquel knows exactly how to get to me.*

After the show was over, Keanu and Raquel joined Kym and Peter for tropical drinks at a nightclub in nearby Wailua, a major commercial center in Kauai County.

"Man, you'll have to show me sometime how you do that with the knives of fire and twirling bit," Keanu said to Peter.

"It comes with lots of practice and trying not to think about it too much." Peter laughed boisterously. "Sure,

I can teach you how to do it. But only if you teach me some of your moves on the basketball court."

Keanu grinned. "Yeah, I can do that." He tried to picture Peter with his large girth doing some moves on the court.

"I remember one time when you dunked on Dwight Howard," Peter said. "You must've caught him napping or something."

Keanu laughed, remembering the occasion. "I just got a step on him and was lucky," he said.

"He's so modest," Kym said, "instead of taking credit where credit is due. Not at all like I expected. Raquel, you'd better hang on to this wonderful man."

Raquel offered a bright smile, cupping her arm beneath Keanu's. "Oh, I intend to."

Keanu put his hand over hers, feeling the heat pass between them. "The feeling is very mutual," he promised, gazing into the depths of her eyes.

"Get a room," joked Kym, making a face.

"We've already got one," Raquel said.

"Then go use it before that energy I see passing between you two explodes and causes this place to catch on fire."

Keanu laughed. "It is getting a bit warm in here," he said, running the back of his hand playfully across his brow. "I thought for a minute there that Peter was gearing up to do his double knife fire routine."

Peter guffawed. "Some fires can start all by themselves with no help from me."

"I'll drink to that." Keanu hoisted his glass as desire for Raquel threatened to engulf him.

"Make that two!" declared Kym.

Raquel and Peter joined in and their glasses clinked.

* * *

The moment they stepped inside their hotel suite, Raquel wasted little time going after what she wanted. After giving Keanu a passionate kiss, she fell to her knees and unzipped his pants. She pulled his manhood out of his underwear. It was erect and throbbing, as turned on by her as she was by it.

She put her mouth over his erection and brought it all the way to the base of her throat, out and back again, before licking the tip. "Are you enjoying this?" she asked, raising her eyes to Keanu's face.

His contorted look of pleasure told her all she needed to know. "Every second, baby," he groaned. "It feels so damned good."

"Then close your eyes and let me continue to pleasure my man."

"Please do," he uttered breathily.

Raquel's nipples tingled with desire as she kissed, licked and fondled Keanu's enormous shaft. It was driving her crazy wanting to have him inside her, but she knew they had all night for intercourse. Now it was all about giving Keanu the exquisite attention he deserved.

She felt Keanu's hands roaming through her hair and heard his breathing quicken as her mouth worked its magic and his rock-hard member quavered from the onslaught. When he had achieved his satisfaction, she got to her feet, wanting him now more than ever.

Raquel began ripping Keanu's clothes off, his firm nakedness making her yearn all the more for his body. Her clothes were discarded just as quickly, and she took the condom from his hands and slid it onto his erection, which showed no sign of abating. She pushed him toward the wall and jumped on him. He grabbed hold of her buttocks and steadied himself as she came down on him. She felt him go deep inside her and contracted around him.

She braced her hands on the wall and started to move up and down him, her core rubbing torturously against his body. Their mouths collided and Raquel sucked on Keanu's lips.

"I want you to make me come," she cried out, her nerve endings on fire.

"I'll give you whatever you want—whenever..." he panted, and squeezed her buttocks while lifting her up and down on his erection.

"Just you, baby," she purred, as the buildup inside her reached a fevered pitch.

Keanu turned them around so Raquel was against the wall. She clamped her legs high around his back as he thrust himself into her hungrily. She met his powerful thrusts with equal abandon, breathing raggedly as she climaxed uncontrollably.

She held on to Keanu's sturdy back while his nearly simultaneous orgasm rippled inside her. Both of them held each other tightly, reveling in their intense passion, wanting to experience every moment of glory together.

When it was over, Keanu let Raquel down, their slick bodies clinging, still hot, and their hearts beating rapidly. It hit Raquel then, as if she hadn't known it before. She was falling in love with Keanu. There was no getting around it. She needed everything he'd given her and so much more.

Did he feel the same way? Could they turn their sexual passion into the love of a lifetime? Or was it expecting too much that she could make it work with an ex-NBA player who was still working on a bad-boy image?

The following Sunday, Keanu invited Victor, Raquel and Lauren, along with his Uncle Sonny and Ashley, to watch a football game in his grand media room. Still fresh on his mind were vivid images of the hot sex between him and Raquel in their hotel room that night in Kauai. He was totally turned on by her take-charge attitude and the way she had demanded whatever she wanted from him. It seemed as if the more they gave one another, the needier they became. Raquel was playing with his emotions like no other woman before her. Keanu wouldn't run away from it. Just the opposite, he was definitely hooked on her and determined to make what they had work for the long run.

Keanu greeted his guests warmly. Especially Raquel, who was casually dressed in cargo shorts, a white sleeveless tank and rounded toe flats. Her hair was tied so it hung on one side across her shoulder. He gave her a kiss and picked up the scent of his own name-brand perfume on her skin.

"You smell wonderful," he whispered in her ear.

"Wonder why?" Her eyes flashed teasingly.

Keanu grinned. "Glad everyone could make it," he said.

"Try and stop me from the chance to see this fabulous house of yours," gushed Lauren.

Keanu grinned. He recalled Raquel telling him how eager she was, as one of his most loyal fans, to be given the grand tour. He was happy to oblige. Especially if it meant earning a few brownie points with Raquel.

"You're always welcome here, Lauren," Keanu told her, wanting Raquel's friend and Victor's girlfriend to feel right at home there.

"Mahalo," Lauren said.

Keanu flashed his teeth. "I'll be happy to show you around later." He put an arm around Raquel. "Right now, the game's about to start."

"Now who did you say was playing?" Raquel asked, cuddling against him.

"The Detroit Lions versus the New Orleans Saints." He had taken a liking to the Lions while playing in Detroit and had become friends with several of the players.

She blushed. "Oh…that's right."

"My money's on the Saints," Victor said confidently.

"I'll be happy to take your money then," said Keanu. "Looking for a big upset by the Lions."

"You're on," his friend stated, tapping him on the back.

Keanu had refreshments waiting as they entered the room, which had a surround sound system and a 65-inch television. He introduced Lauren to his uncle and Ashley, who had already claimed their seats.

"Aloha," Ashley said to everyone.

"It's 'bout time Keanu started to invite friends over and bring some life back into the house," Sonny said, grinning from ear to ear.

"I've been riding him about doing that very thing," Victor said. "He's finally starting to listen."

Keanu laughed, pleased at the thought of turning his private oasis into a social place. Now that he had Raquel in his life, he felt more inspired to have gatherings there and hoped it could become a regular thing.

"We're going to have a great time," he promised, adding with a laugh, "but *only* if the Lions come away victorious."

Sharing a bowl of popcorn with Raquel, Keanu tried to focus on the game, but was more drawn to his girlfriend and thinking of the wicked things they could be doing instead.

She picked up on it, whispering to him, "Um, let's try and keep our mind on the game."

He grinned naughtily, whispering back, "Can I help it if that's damned near impossible when we could be playing our own private game?"

"You'll get your wish later," she promised, putting a piece of popcorn in his mouth. "Now watch."

Keanu accepted the compromise, suppressing his carnal thoughts till they could be alone. He ate more popcorn contentedly.

By halftime, with the Lions nursing a precarious three-point lead, Keanu, Raquel and Lauren went to the kitchen for more refreshments, but took a detour to check out the house and grounds.

They made their way from exquisite room to exquisite room, stopping briefly in Keanu's large private study, where he had mahogany floor-to-ceiling bookcases lined with books he'd collected over the years, many autographed by bestselling writer friends. From there they stepped onto a trellised lanai, one of several covered patios on the estate, and admired the magnificent view it afforded them.

"This place is utterly amazing," Lauren said.

"That's what I've been telling him," Raquel said.

"It's pretty cool," Keanu allowed, thinking how much more amazing it would be if Raquel lived there with him as his wife and soul mate. That way they could always be around one another to have fun, make love and hang out, instead of having to go back and forth between residences. The idea of marriage was a big step for him, as was the concept of truly loving a woman. But with Raquel, both seemed right. He would be happy to share his life, money and estate with her. Would she be willing to leave behind her place in Waikiki to move in with him, even if she wasn't quite ready to walk down the aisle? Keanu imagined Raquel might even want to redecorate the house to feel more at home.

Or was it a direction she did not see them headed in as lovers and business partners? He didn't want her to feel pressured in any way. But Keanu also wanted Raquel to know just how serious he was about her and what she meant to him. In his mind, that meant doing whatever was necessary to make it abundantly clear that he intended for their relationship to go long and far.

"And to think this could be all yours, girl," Lauren gushed. She and Raquel had slipped away before the second half of the game under the guise of going to the bathroom.

"I'm sure lots of other women have thought the same thing," Raquel responded dryly. "Only to be in for a rude awakening."

"Hey, you're not the same as other women Keanu has dated," insisted Lauren, while they looked out the window at the ocean. "I've read or heard about many of them and I didn't get the impression that any had truly hooked him. Not the way you have."

"Not sure I have him totally hooked," Raquel said.

"But we do seem to be embarking on something special."

"Duh, you think?" Lauren batted her lashes. "If not for you, I would never have found myself in the home of my favorite basketball player. And he's been so nice about it—treating me as more than just a goo-goo, ga-ga fan."

Raquel chuckled. "Seems like you've got the inside track with Keanu in more ways than one."

Lauren grinned. "Maybe, but you've got the ins with him in the way that counts most, girlfriend—matters close to the heart."

"We'll see about that," was all Raquel would say on the subject. Just how close to Keanu's heart had she gotten? There was no doubt that she had him totally enthralled below the waist and had also gained his respect as an image consultant. But whether or not this all translated to real love was still open for debate.

"I can just see you living here," Lauren said. "Can you imagine the parties you could give?"

Raquel laughed. "You're crazy. First of all, I'm not making any plans to sell my place in Waikiki, even if it's for an obvious upgrade. Keanu and I have not talked about living together here or anywhere else. As for parties, I'm not too big on those and all the work you have to go through. And Keanu is supposed to be getting away from that type of life, not embracing it, whether I'm in his life or not."

Lauren pushed her, making a playful face. "Will you lighten up? I know you're not married to the man and his money yet and are not wild about parties. Doesn't mean a girl—make that two girls—can't dream a little, does it?"

"Dream on," Raquel told her, smiling. "I'll just stick to reality at the moment. Whatever the future holds, I'll deal with it then." In the meantime, she intended to hang on to the strong feelings she had for Keanu and the belief that they were moving in the right direction in their relationship.

She took Lauren's hand. "I think we'd better get back in the theater room before they start to miss us."

"If you insist," Lauren muttered.

"There will be other times for us to enjoy Keanu's house—and his pool," Raquel promised, confident that at the very least, he had opened up his home to her and her friends.

Chapter 11

A few days later, Raquel had lunch at her mother's house. It gave Raquel a good excuse to talk about her growing feelings for Keanu. They ate out on the covered lanai, sitting on wicker chairs around an octagonal table.

"I'm glad you found some time to spend with your mother what with your busy schedule these days," complained Davetta, stirring cream into her coffee.

"I think we've both been pretty busy," Raquel said, taking a bite from her corned beef sandwich. Her mother still worked full-time, in addition to her volunteer work at the church and with the Red Cross. Not to mention that she spent much of her free time with Sean.

"I suppose. Anyway, you're here now."

Raquel smiled. "You can call me anytime."

"That works both ways," Davetta reminded her.

"I get it." Raquel's brow furrowed guiltily. "Guess I'm sometimes too involved in my own little dramas to remember that."

Davetta leaned forward. "Would one of those dramas happen to be Keanu Bailey?"

As if she couldn't guess. "Yes, as a matter of fact," admitted Raquel.

Davetta's eyes narrowed. "You haven't let that handsome young man get away, have you?"

"No, Mom, I haven't." Raquel took a breath.

"Thank goodness. Even Sean thinks he's a catch, and he's impressed that Keanu seems like he's really ready to settle down with the right woman and bring some cute little ones into the world."

"We're still seeing each other," Raquel reiterated, putting a fork in her salad.

"And..." her mother probed.

"And, I'm falling hard for him." She came right out with it.

Davetta smiled. "From what Keanu had to say on Thanksgiving, I think the feelings are mutual."

Raquel concurred, even if he had yet to say the magical words to her that she wanted to hear. "We seem to be hitting it off really well," she conceded and thought about how they had made love for an hour after watching the Lions beat the Saints the other day.

"Then what's the problem?" Davetta asked.

"The problem is twofold," Raquel said. "One is that I'm dying to tell Keanu that I'm in love. At least I'm pretty sure that's what I'm feeling, and I don't take it lightly. But I need to know that we are on the same track, beyond our sexual chemistry—"

Too much information. Better leave it at that.

"Let him tell you first," Davetta surprised her by saying.

Raquel's eyes grew wide. "Really?"

"Your father was pretty stubborn about keeping his true emotions to himself when we started dating," she said thoughtfully. "But I could be pretty stubborn too. I wasn't about to pour my heart out and reveal just how much I loved him only to scare the poor man off. Worse would have been to give in to my feelings without being dead certain that he felt exactly the same way—and not just in the bedroom. Otherwise it'll never work. I'm also old-fashioned when it comes to that sort of thing. I believe the man should step forward first—even a wealthy, retired ballplayer, whom I'd love to have as a son-in-law and the father of my grandchildren."

"Wow!" Raquel laughed. Could Davetta be any more blunt about what she wanted? "So does that mean you're waiting for Sean to make his move first?"

Davetta smiled. "We have a pretty good thing going, but neither of us is ready to move in that direction right now. We're just enjoying each other's company and will see where it leads."

"I see." Raquel was surprised that her old-fashioned mother was satisfied with simply enjoying the company of a man over a commitment of love and marriage. *Guess times are changing. Dad's hold on her is obviously hard for her to let go of.* She drank some water. "And to think, I thought you had spilled your guts to Dad first, before he manned up and told you he loved you."

"Believe me, I thought about it on more than one occasion," Davetta said, nibbling around the corners of her sandwich. "But in the end, I stuck to my guns, just as my mother had in waiting for your grandfather to do the right thing."

"So you think I should just sit back and be patient with Keanu till he declares his undying love for me and asks for my hand in marriage—if, in fact, he ever does?" Raquel asked.

"I do," Davetta responded with a nod. "But the way that man couldn't keep his eyes or hands off you, I'm guessing that he's just waiting for the right time to tell you how he feels."

"That brings me to my other problem…" Raquel said.

"Which is?" Davetta stared at her with her mouth slightly open.

"Even if Keanu were to express his love for me, can he really put the playboy lifestyle of a single basketball player behind him? Or am I deluding myself?"

"No, you're not deluding yourself, child." Davetta tasted her coffee. "Whatever he did previously doesn't matter. People can change. As I told you before, often it takes the right woman to bring about a changed man."

"You really think so?" Raquel thought about the women Keanu had bedded before her and the active social life he had. What if he grew bored with her and had a yearning to repeat history? Where would that leave her and the strong emotions she had for him?

Davetta looked at her. "Excuse me, but isn't that why Keanu hired you in the first place—to help change his image?"

"Yes," admitted Raquel. "And he's doing that, by all accounts. However—"

"Then trust your own skills as well as his good intentions," her mother cut in. "Whatever Keanu did with his life during his colorful NBA days is history."

"So he says."

"And has he done anything to make you feel otherwise?" Davetta asked.

"No." Raquel thought about Keanu's jerk of a friend, Derek. Should a man be judged by the company he kept? Or on his own merits and current behavior? She decided the latter.

Her mother agreed. "Then there's your answer," she said. "Give the man a chance to do right by you and by himself. Heaven knows how hard it's been for you to meet someone who can make you smile. Not to mention fall in love. Don't let doubts and rumors ruin a good thing with so much potential for you both."

"You're right," Raquel said, grabbing a raisin cookie from a plate. "I'll try to keep my eyes on the prize and not look for things that aren't there." She sighed and wondered if that was easier said than done. "I'll just sit back and wait for Keanu to make the first move in declaring his feelings." *I only hope they're the same as mine for him.*

On Thursday, Raquel gave a seminar on polishing one's professional image. It had been scheduled for two months now, but was apropos for Keanu, whom she'd invited to attend. He was quick to accept, believing in her skills as a consultant and coach.

Dressed in a black two-button stretch jacket with a notched collar and matching flared skirt, Raquel was the image of professionalism. Her long hair was in a loose chignon and, as always, she wore just enough makeup to accentuate her natural coloring. Raquel stood before the audience of twenty men and women, making use of the blackboard behind her as she went into her professional spiel.

"There are six P's that are essential in successful marketing," she began. "Presence, personality, presentation, packaging, potential and persuasion. If you can master these, every one of you can turn weak marketability into a strong plan for selling yourself. Now let's go over these one by one...."

Twenty minutes later, Raquel had cleared the blackboard and moved on to her next topic.

"Next is media savvy," Raquel said, taking a measured breath. "Most of you, I'm sure, recognize the value in receiving positive media coverage in this digital age. Conversely, negative press coverage can not only hurt your public persona, but also adversely affect your personal image." She eyed Keanu, who nodded. "The good news is that a negative can be turned into a positive by transforming a damaged or less than appealing image into one that is wholesome, uplifting and even targeted. We'll go through these and other aspects of media savoir faire that will give you the basics in dealing with this area of personal marketing—"

When the session was over, Raquel breathed a sigh of relief that she had been able to stay on message in spite of feeling the heat from Keanu's overpowering presence. But it had also served to motivate her to be herself during the seminar, and she hoped it would be another piece of the puzzle for improving all areas of his own public image.

"You were amazing," Keanu told her, offering his hand to shake as if he were just another attendee.

Raquel smiled professionally and shook his hand.

"Why thank you, Mr. Bailey." She nearly melted from the searing heat of his gaze bearing down on her face. "I thought the seminar might be beneficial to you."

"Absolutely." He grinned coolly. "I learned a great deal, thanks to you."

"Good. It's all just part of what I do."

"And you do it very well," he told her.

"*Mahalo nui loa* for the compliment," Raquel thanked him very much as she closed her briefcase. "I'll try not to let it go to my head."

Keanu looked at her. "Speaking of which, I love the way you have your hair done up like that."

"It's one of my professional looks," she said, pushing away an errant strand of hair.

"You should wear it that way more often," he suggested.

"If you like."

"I like it—and everything else about you, Ms. Deneuve."

Raquel flushed hotly, mindful that a few other attendees were still milling about. "I'll keep that in mind."

"Can I buy you lunch?" Keanu asked smoothly.

"I'd like that," she responded, feeling hunger pangs. Along with a spasm of desire for the man who had, perhaps unbeknownst to him, stolen her heart and soul.

Keanu picked a quiet place on Oahu's eastern shore off Kalanianaole Highway to dine. He was still thinking about the seminar and Raquel's tips as they sat in the Hawaiian restaurant. Perhaps the best thing his agent had ever done in the decade they had been together had been hooking him up with Raquel. Not only had she been an astute image consultant, but she was a very beautiful woman who could keep up with him in and out of the bedroom.

They had cast aside inhibitions and mixed business with pleasure. Now he couldn't imagine his life without the sexy, gorgeous, soulful woman who made his heart beat faster whenever he touched her. If things went his way, he might never have to find out what his future would be like if Raquel wasn't around to share it with him.

"Got some news for you." He got Raquel's attention, as she seemed deep in thought while slicing through her grilled pork tenderloin. "I spoke to the NBA commissioner and it looks like I will take part in the Basketball Without Borders program next summer."

"Why, that's terrific!" Raquel smiled. "Do you know where you'll be headed?"

"Not yet," Keanu told her, putting a piece of filet mignon in his mouth. "What I do know is that I'd like you there with me."

Her eyes twinkled. "Is that an invitation?"

"Definitely. I also remember it's something you said you wanted to do."

"I meant it," she said.

"So do I," he said. "I think together we'd make a great team with the program."

She smiled. "I couldn't agree more."

"And it would also give us a chance to explore some other part of the world."

"That could be fun," Raquel said.

Keanu sipped his chardonnay. "I'm sure it would be."

She looked at him. "So I take it that means you expect what we have to be long lasting?"

"Yes." He met her gaze. "Don't you?"

"I want that," she said. "It's just that we haven't talked much about what we expect out of our relationship for the future."

Keanu reached out and touched her hand. "I expect the future will be very bright for us, baby," he said. "I know I want you in my life."

"I want that too." She curled her fingers around his. "As you said, we make a great team."

He smiled genuinely. "The greatest from where I'm sitting."

Her mouth curved sensually at the corners. "Maybe we should take this somewhere a little more private."

"Maybe we should." He just wanted to get Raquel naked, kiss her all over and make love till the wee hours of the morning. He knew that their passion could only lead to more passion, until any notion of a life apart would be unbearable.

Finally back at Keanu's estate, he and Raquel retreated to the bedroom and immediately stripped down and lunged at each other. Keanu had his face between Raquel's legs, which cradled his head. He slipped his tongue inside her, feeling her wetness that was thick and wonderful. He flicked his tongue back and forth across her clitoris, feeling her body tense from the exquisite pleasure. Breathing in her erotic, womanly scent, Keanu was turned on even more, loving this part of their intimacy.

Raquel flipped and enveloped his manhood in her mouth, teasing the tip unmercifully. It was all Keanu could do not to explode on the spot. Instead he fought to suppress the urge, wanting to extend their dual pleasure for as long as possible. Or at least until Raquel's body told him that her orgasm had come full force from his focused persuasion. He continued to relentlessly pleasure her with his mouth as she pleasured him, both moaning and shaking as the buildup to sexual release grew stronger with each passing moment.

When the surge of heightened desire reached its pinnacle, Keanu clutched Raquel's thighs and brought her over the top, even as she caused him to groan with orgasmic joy. They lay upside down for a few minutes to catch their breath and soak in the swell of sweet satisfaction before turning right side up and kissing each other's mouth rapaciously.

Two hours later, Keanu broke away from a spine-tingling kiss to rapidly put on a condom over his erection before coming back to Raquel's waiting body and full lips. He slid deep inside her and she locked her legs around his, her breasts heaving against his muscular chest, arms tightly wound around his neck, their lips embraced in carnal kissing as they made love with a passion.

A cry erupted from Raquel's mouth when her climax set in. "Ooh…Keanu, this is too good, too powerful, too satisfying…"

Keanu felt her strong contractions as he propelled himself deeper inside of her, while their bodies, slick with perspiration, clung together.

"You're killing me with desire to own every inch of your body, baby," Keanu growled as his heart beat wildly.

"So own it," demanded Raquel. "Own it now…now… now—"

Raquel's voice became a long moan as her orgasm rolled forth, causing her to shake uncontrollably. Keanu held her closely, kissing her maddeningly. His climax came moments later, and they bounced on the bed with each thrust as both concentrated on achieving earth-shattering gratification.

Afterward, Keanu gave Raquel a scrumptious kiss, feeling so complete and relaxed with her. She had given him more than he ever thought possible as a lover and a woman. He could not imagine another woman ever measuring up to Raquel or another man wanting her as much as he did.

He needed to let her know how he felt about her and hope the feeling was not only mutual, but also one that Raquel never wanted to let go of.

Chapter 12

Floating on cloud nine after she and Keanu made love, Raquel decided to take the rest of the day off. She had hoped that, as they lay cuddled, their naked bodies pressed together perfectly with her back to him, Keanu might utter the words Raquel wanted to hear. Instead he was silent. Maybe he thought that his actions spoke louder than words, but they did not as far as she was concerned. She needed to hear them spoken in plain English. Was this an indication that the player in Keanu was still unable to commit his heart to one woman?

Am I getting in too deep with a man who wants me, but only on his own terms? Or am I just too impatient and want someone who isn't quite sure of his feelings for me?

She felt Keanu's lips on her shoulder. "You're the best I've ever had," he murmured.

"You're sure about that?" she asked, wondering if he was referring to her or the sex.

He kissed her again. "I've never been so sure about anything in my life."

"So what are you saying?" Raquel needed to know. She turned over to look at him.

"Let's go take a walk on the beach," he said.

"Now?"

"Yeah, now," he said gazing into her eyes. "It's secluded, and it's a gorgeous afternoon for a stroll."

As much as she loved the beach, Raquel would've preferred they stay there and talk. She had a feeling that Keanu was trying to divert his thoughts to something less serious and threatening to his way of life.

"Fine," Raquel said. She knew that she was hooked on him no matter what happened. But if he was going to break her heart, she'd rather he did it now before her feelings for him became so ingrained that it would be impossible for her to walk away.

Keanu led Raquel through his private entrance to the beach. In all the times he had taken a walk on this beach, none had been as momentous as this occasion, when he was finally ready to lay his feelings on the line. What would she say? Did she still see him as an ex-athlete who could never be committed to one woman?

He held Raquel's hand as they walked barefoot in the sand with soft waves rolling across their feet. Keanu said, "I love being out here with you."

She smiled tentatively at him. "I feel the same way."

"Really?"

"Do you doubt it?" Her lips twisted. "Isn't it obvious how comfortable I've grown being around you?"

Keanu grinned. "Yeah, it is." *Comfortable is a good start.* He stopped walking and faced her. It was time to just come out with it and see how she reacted. He took a breath. "I've fallen in love with you...."

Her eyes blazed. "What did you say?"

He stared into her gorgeous eyes intently. "I'm in love with you."

"You're serious?"

"I have never been more serious." Keanu's heart skipped a beat. He gently held her cheeks and kissed her lips. "I love you, Raquel."

She licked her mouth. "So, what took you so long?"

A crooked grin spread across his lips. "I wanted to wait for the right time."

"You mean not in bed after we were both a little crazy and off balance from having sex?"

"Exactly," he said with a smile. "Or any other time that wasn't perfect."

Raquel caressed his cheek. "I've fallen in love with you, too."

"Have you?" Keanu ignored the ocean water that splashed onto his feet, wanting to know that her words were sincere.

"Yes," she said.

"Since when?" he asked.

"Since before now."

He raised a brow. "But you never said anything."

"I wasn't going to say anything," Raquel told him, "until I knew you felt the same way."

Keanu held her gaze, seeing the light in it. He broke

into a grin. "So that's the way you wanted to play it, huh?"

She smiled. "I wanted to be on a winning team."

He laughed and wrapped his arms around her waist. "You'll always be a winner with me."

Raquel kissed him. "Are you sure you can handle being in love with just one woman?"

His expression turned serious. "Yes, if it's the right woman. You."

"And you're really ready to put your bad-boy days behind you?"

He pulled her closer. "What do you think? Isn't that what I'm paying you for?"

A tiny smile played on her lips. "You're paying me to help reshape your image. It'll take more than my business skills to keep your heart in the right place."

"That's where your personal skills come into play," Keanu said. "They are keeping my heart and head in the right place—with you and only you."

He leaned over and gave her a deep kiss as though to prove his point. She turned pliable to his touch.

Raquel broke their lip lock. "Okay, I believe you."

"Prove it," he challenged her.

Her lashes fluttered. "You mean you want us to go back inside and jump each other's bones some more?"

The thought had certainly crossed Keanu's mind, as he never seemed to be able to get enough of Raquel. But at the moment he was thinking on another track.

"Marry me," he told her in earnest.

Raquel lifted her chin. "Are you seriously proposing?"

"Yeah, I am." It was a spur of the moment thing for

him, though this was something he had been deliberating for a while. But the timing seemed so right.

"Is there a ring?" She looked at him as if expecting him to pull it out of a pocket.

"No, not yet," he had to admit. "Just say yes and I'll get you two damned rings. I want you to be my wife, live in my house and share the joys of my life."

Raquel swallowed and put her hand on his chest. "Can I think about it?"

His eyes grew wide. "You need to think about marrying the man you say you love?"

"No, it's my way of saying I want *you* to take some time to think about it," she said.

"I don't follow." Keanu's brow furrowed.

She sighed. "Since you proposed without having an engagement ring in hand, it tells me that this was an impromptu decision. I don't doubt that you love me and please don't doubt my love for you. But we come from different places in life, and I just want you to be sure that you are fully committed to spending the rest of your life with me as your wife. I won't settle for anything less."

"I never expected you would," he told her. "You're the real deal for me and I want us—"

Raquel cut him off by putting a finger on his lips. "If that's the case, then you won't mind taking a little more time to be secure in your feelings, for both our sakes. Ask me again once you've done that, and then I'll give you my answer."

She lifted up on her toes and kissed him, opening her mouth to his and letting Keanu taste her tongue. It aroused him, and he wanted to take her back to bed. Was this a test to see if he was really true to her and not simply biding his time till a better woman came along? Or did it go deeper than that?

Keanu continued the kiss she had started, allowing his mind to drift to powerful sexual impulses. Yet he craved so much more from the woman who he had hoped would be his wife, as well as his best friend and lover.

The following morning, Raquel used the elliptical machine in the fitness center at Waikiki Place. Though her limbs were still tired from the sexual workout she'd gotten with Keanu yesterday, she willed herself to stick to her near-daily routine. At least while she lived in her own place. Raquel imagined that if she and Keanu were to marry and live in his home, she would replace some of her current exercises with swimming and basketball. Not to mention more frequent sex, for if they were sharing the same space, she believed they would find it nearly impossible to keep their hands and bodies off each other.

Did I lose my mind when I turned down his proposal? What was I thinking?

But she hadn't lost her mind at all. Yes, she had longed for him to tell her he loved her. And she would like nothing better than to become his wife. But she saw no reason to do this the wrong way. It was obvious that Keanu's proposal was on the spur of the moment. Or fresh off of the sexual passion between them.

She still believed in being proposed to with an engagement ring in hand, especially when she had no doubt he could afford one. By delaying her answer, she wanted to give Keanu not only the opportunity to do it the proper way next time, but to give them a period to be sure this was what they both truly wanted.

Raquel fought the strain in her arms and legs while continuing to move. She knew that she loved Keanu and was ready to get married at this point in her life. But was he? Though he'd obviously done much to repair his bad boy, partying hard image, was he really prepared to put all other women behind him forever and be her husband for a lifetime? Anything less would not be enough for her, as she didn't want to end up as another ex-wife of an athlete once the passion had died down or a younger, prettier woman captured his attention.

What about children? She and Keanu had really never talked about children in specific terms. How many kids did he want? One, two, three, or more? Maybe he didn't want any. Raquel had always thought that having one or two little ones might be nice.

These were the type of things she and Keanu needed to talk about up front to make sure they were on the same page or, at the very least, reading the same book.

After exercising for forty minutes, Raquel took a hot shower and dressed for work. When she checked her cell phone for messages from Keanu, she found there were none.

Should I be concerned or am I looking for something that isn't there?

She gave him the benefit of the doubt. He'd agreed to take some time to think things through and maybe that was part of the process. She could only hope.

Keanu made morning calls to his agent, lawyer, financial adviser and accountant. The fact that he had kept a relatively low profile since retiring from the

NBA, along with the improvements to his image, had made him more attractive to companies for potential endorsements. Or so his agent, Richard Brock, had told him.

All the credit went to Raquel, as far as Keanu was concerned. She had done wonders to point him in the right direction, and the results were apparent. He was totally satisfied with their professional relationship. However, it was where things stood between them on a personal level that left him uncertain.

In spite of the fact that they had made love after Raquel had failed to give him an answer to his proposal, Keanu still felt stung by it. Why was Raquel stalling? Did she not really love him the way she claimed to? Or was marrying a well-known athlete more than she could handle?

Keanu carried those burning questions with him as he found his uncle on the lanai, sitting on an Adirondack chaise longue munching on papaya fruit.

"Hey, Unc," he said.

"Aloha *kakahiaka*." Sonny crinkled his eyes after saying good morning in Hawaiian. "What's up?"

Keanu sighed. His uncle had always been good at sensing when something was bothering him. Why should this be any different?

He grabbed a banana from a bowl of fruit and sat on a cedar glider chair. After a moment or two, Keanu said, "I told Raquel I loved her."

Sonny looked at him with a cocked brow. "I figured you were headed in that direction. How did she take it?"

"She said she loved me too." Keanu thought back to that instant and how good it felt to confirm what his instincts had already believed.

"You don't look like a man who's found love with a beautiful young woman," Sonny said.

"I asked her to marry me," he told him.

"And?"

"She said she needed to think about it and wanted me to do the same," Keanu said glumly.

"And that's a bad thing?" Sonny gazed at him.

"You tell me." Keanu told him about Raquel's response.

"Frankly, I think it was a wise move on her part," Sonny said. "She didn't turn you down, she just gave you both more time to make sure what you feel for each other can survive this first test."

Keanu's eyes narrowed quizzically. "Test?"

"Sure. Every point of contention in a relationship is a test. I should know that as well as anyone, having been through a few in my time." Sonny drank some fruit juice. "Raquel seems like a pretty smart woman. I'm sure she loves you, just as you love her. But put yourself in her shoes. Your reputation as a ladies' man is still out there. If I were her, I'd want to take a little extra time too before accepting your proposal so I don't end up getting burned."

"I wouldn't do that to her," Keanu said, frowning. "I'm not the same man I used to be. Not now that Raquel has come into my life."

"Yeah, I can see that," Sonny told him. "I'm sure Raquel can, too. But you've got to cut her some slack here. You're a big-time basketball star who hired her to help rid yourself of old demons. Now you're ready to marry her. Just take the time to think long and hard about this, and let her do the same. Think about what it means to be married and tied down to one woman for the long haul, when decisions are made jointly and not just by you. Think about having a family of your own for the first time, how many kids you want, and if you're up to the challenge of being a husband and daddy. It's damned hard, let me tell you."

"I know," Keanu conceded, lowering his eyes thoughtfully.

"I'm not trying to get you to rethink your desire to marry the woman," said Sonny. "Quite the opposite. I'd like nothing better than to welcome Raquel into the family, as she seems like the first woman I can recall who has truly made you happy for longer than the blink of an eye. Hell, you could even have the wedding here. Make it something really special. But just do as she suggested and ask her again later once you've both let it sink in."

"All right, Unc." Keanu smiled. "I guess I'm guilty of overthinking this and trying to rush something that doesn't need to be rushed." Keanu finished the banana. "Okay, we'll do it her way."

Sonny stood and patted him on the shoulder. "No, boy, you're doing it the correct way for both of you. I'm sure next time you'll get the answer you want to hear."

Keanu rose above his uncle. "I hope so. Thanks for the advice and words of wisdom."

Sonny nodded. "I wouldn't be much of an uncle if you couldn't count on me in that regard, would I?"

Keanu smiled. "I guess not."

He left the house and hopped in his car to drive around, putting on some jazz music. Apart from enjoying the sights and sounds of Honolulu, Keanu found this was a good way to relax and ponder the twists and turns his life had taken.

* * *

"I didn't realize things had gotten that serious between you two," Kym told Raquel after dropping by her office.

Raquel blushed as they sat there, having spilled the beans about Keanu's marriage proposal to her friend. "It all happened so quickly, practically before I realized what was going on," she explained.

"So do you love him?" Kym asked.

"Yes," Raquel admitted. "Imagine that, I've actually fallen in love with someone instead of merely going through the motions of dating men, knowing it was going nowhere."

"It's about time," Kym said. "I was beginning to think that I was the only one of my friends willing to live the married life. Welcome to the club."

Raquel almost hated to tell her the rest of the story. "Actually, I may not be quite ready to join the club yet. I told Keanu I wanted to think about it."

"What?" Kym's eyes grew in surprise. "How did that go over?"

Raquel had to ask herself the same question. "I'm sure it wasn't quite what he expected to hear," she said. "But I believe he respected my answer once I told him why."

"The man's gorgeous, loaded and loves you enough to want you as his wife," Kym said. "What is there to think about? Or am I being too nosy here?"

Raquel forced a smile. "No, you're not," she told her. She had to expect there might be this type of reaction. "It's not about Keanu's good looks and certainly not about his money. I'm sure he does love me. I just want him to be certain I'm the one he wants to be with for the rest of our lives."

"There are no guarantees, Raquel. Marriage takes some work, but if two people love each other from the start, isn't it worth the risk?"

"Yes, of course," Raquel answered defensively. "The risk may be greater though when it involves an ex-athlete who has always been single and is used to coming and going as he pleases. I'm not saying that Keanu isn't sincere in his proposal. I just want him to contemplate what it means to be married to a strong woman and ask me again, be it next week, next month, or next year, and we'll go from there."

Kym leaned back. "I have to admit, I know nothing about the dynamics of professional athletes and their track record for failed relationships and marriages. But from what little I know about Keanu, he seems like a really great guy who's pretty hung up on you. I haven't followed his career much in the NBA, not like Peter has. For that matter, I haven't even kept up with the latest gossip on him. But my guess is that he asked you to marry him because he truly does love you and thinks you can make this work. Of course, I am a hopeless romantic, so I could be way off base here...."

"You are a hopeless romantic, Kym," Raquel said with a laugh. "And Peter's lucky to have you as his wife. I see where you're coming from. Keanu is a great guy and I'm pretty hung up on him too. I just hope he realizes that and proposes again with a ring and the knowledge of what it means to have a wife."

"I'm sure he will ask for your hand in marriage again," Kym said. "When two people belong together as you seem to, everything usually works out in the end. If not, then it probably wasn't meant to be."

Raquel bristled at the notion that what she and Keanu had started was not meant to end with marriage, family and a loving life together. But she was also a realist. Some men expected women to bend to their will as though they had no mind of their own. She didn't believe this to be the case with Keanu. If it were, he was not the man for her in the long run. If he respected her and understood that her hesitation was not at all a reflection on him, but rather a pause to give them both an opportunity to either back away or move forward wholeheartedly, then Raquel was sure that she had not lost her man or his love.

Chapter 13

Raquel waited a full day before getting up the nerve to call her mother to fill her in about where things stood with Keanu.

She'll probably have a conniption when I tell her. Might as well just get it over with.

"Hi, Mom," Raquel said.

"Hold on and let me get Sean off the line," Davetta told her.

Normally Raquel would have told her she'd call back another time, but since her mother and Sean often spoke on the phone for hours at a time, that wasn't an option.

A moment later, Davetta was back. "Sean and I were just talking about Christmas. I assume we're still on for dinner with Keanu and his family, right?"

"As far as I know," Raquel said. They hadn't talked about it lately, but she had no reason to believe Keanu would back out unless he planned to end their relationship. That was something Raquel didn't even want to think about as a remote possibility, though it was impossible to dismiss the thought altogether. Maybe Keanu was rethinking his invitation. But she wouldn't go there. They were still seeing each other. She just needed to know that he had other women totally out of his system and was ready to make a full commitment to her that would stand the test of time. One small bump in the road shouldn't change how they felt about one another at the end of the day.

"Wonderful," Davetta said. "Beyond that, we'll be spending time with Sean's family and, of course, by ourselves."

"I'm happy to hear that." Raquel swallowed thickly, knowing it was time to stop beating around the bush. "Keanu told me he loved me and asked me to marry him. But before you start planning the wedding, I told him that I wanted us to take some time to think about it."

Now she'll let me have it for putting my future with a handsome and rich man at risk.

"That was smart of you," Davetta said.

"It was?"

"Of course," her mother replied. "First of all, I'm happy that Keanu finally got around to sharing his feelings of love with you. I'm even happier that he asked you to marry him. But that doesn't mean you need to respond immediately, or that by not doing so means you don't love him just as much. It's a good thing to let it sink in for both of you, so there are no regrets later."

"*Mahalo* for saying that, Mom," Raquel told her, realizing her mother was much more rational about matters of the heart than she'd given her credit for.

"I'm only telling you what any mother who loves her daughter would. I want to see you happy without sacrificing who you are in the process," Davetta said. "Keanu knows what a good catch you are. He won't give that up easily. The man loves you as much, if not more, than you love him."

A laugh slipped from Raquel's mouth. "Oh, Mom, you truly are a hopeless romantic, you know that?"

"Your father used to always tell me that. I never disputed it, and I'm too old to start now."

"You'll never be too old to be romantic," Raquel told her. "And I'm following in your footsteps."

"I can see that and I'm very proud of you," Davetta said. "You and Keanu belong together and I'm sure that's exactly how this will play out."

"We'll see," Raquel said, leaving it at that as she hung up.

Lying fully clothed on her bed, she couldn't help but think about the last time Keanu had been lying there with her. Not to mention what they were doing in bed, which was often anything but sleep. She could still smell him, which turned her on. She could not imagine any other man being able to ease her fears of being hurt or falling deeply in love like Keanu had managed to do.

But whether or not that translated into matrimony and all that accompanied it was still up in the air. Raquel knew only what she deserved in a marriage and husband if and when the time ever came to walk down the aisle.

I want the glittering engagement and wedding rings,

the big once-in-a-lifetime wedding, the happily ever
after and a man who worships me as much as I do him.

Was that asking too much? She didn't believe so.

Keanu was sitting by the pool catching some rays
and sipping from a bottle of Colt 45 malt liquor when
his phone rang. His nostrils flared when the caller ID
showed that it was his backstabbing friend Derek Gilmore. He had resisted the urge to call Derek ever since
he hit on Raquel, figuring some things were better
left unsaid. Obviously Derek just wouldn't leave well
enough alone.

"Hey, what's up, bro?" Derek said nonchalantly.

"Don't 'what's up, bro' me," Keanu said with an edge
to his tone. "You have a hell of a nerve calling me after
what you did."

"What did I do?" Derek asked, dumbfounded.

Keanu sat up. "You know damn well what you did!
You tried to put the moves on my girlfriend behind my
back."

"Oh that…" Derek muttered with a sigh.

"Yeah, that!" blared Keanu. "I thought we were
friends, man. But you came into my town and crossed
a line that a *real* friend never would."

"I know this may sound lame," Derek began, "but I
had too much to drink and did something really stupid.
I apologize to you and your girl."

"It does sound lame, and I don't accept your apol-
ogy," Keanu said flatly.

He thought about how Raquel had been willing to
forgive, if not forget. He knew that sometimes people
did stupid things—especially when inebriated. Did that
excuse poor behavior? No, but as part of his new image

of keeping a cool head and letting bygones be bygones, it made sense to just let it go.

"We've been buddies for a while," Derek said. "I don't want to lose our friendship because of one dumb mistake. I disrespected someone you're into, and it shouldn't have happened. If I hadn't had one drink too many and could do it over again, I would."

Keanu decided to take the high road and believe that Derek was being sincere in trying to make things right. "Look, why don't we just forget it," he said.

"So we're cool?" Derek asked.

Keanu paused thoughtfully before giving him the benefit of the doubt. "Yeah, man," he told him.

"*Mahalo.* I learned that word on my Hawaiian cruise," Derek said.

"*A'ole pilikia,*" Keanu responded with amusement. "That means no problem."

He kept the conversation brief, not quite ready to completely pick up where they had left off in their friendship. As far as he was concerned, Derek would have to earn back his respect before being considered a true buddy again.

After he got off the phone, Keanu decided to call Raquel. It had been a few days since they last spoke, and he missed her like crazy. But he needed time to digest everything and felt like it might not be a bad idea to give her a little space. She probably needed it to contemplate their future as much as he did. Nothing about his feelings for Raquel had changed, but he couldn't let that cloud his judgment about what his next move should be. The important thing was that Raquel was a special woman who did it for him in every way and that meant more to him than he could say.

If she feels the same way, then as Unc told me, everything else is simply part of the process.

Keanu felt uplifted by that thought as the phone rang. She answered almost immediately.

"Hey," he said, keeping his voice steady.

"Hi." Her voice shook.

"Missed you."

"Missed you, too," she told him.

It was what Keanu wanted to hear. He thought about their last outing, which ended with them making love before she left him wanting more and feeling a little uncertain.

"I just got a call from Derek," Keanu said, wondering how she would react.

"Oh…" She made a humming noise. "What did he have to say for himself, if anything?"

"Only that he was drunk and that he made a damned fool out of himself." Keanu sighed. "He apologized to you and me."

"That's good enough for me," she said simply.

"Is it?" he asked.

"Yes. It's over and done with. No need to dwell on the past."

Keanu tasted the beer. "That's what I thought."

"I understand that some men are like that, drunk or not, athlete or not."

Keanu could hardly argue against that reality. "I suppose some men are dogs," he said. "Present company excluded."

"True." She chuckled. "But it doesn't mean I'm ready to invite Derek over for dinner anytime soon if he comes back to Honolulu."

Keanu laughed. "Neither am I," he assured her.

"Glad to know we see eye to eye on some things," she said good-naturedly.

Keanu looked at his pool and thought about how much fun they had getting wet in there. "We see eye to eye on a lot of things."

"You think?"

"Yeah. Guess that's why we make such a good couple."

"Nice point." She paused. "I never felt we didn't make a good couple. You know that, right?"

"Yes," Keanu replied thoughtfully. "We're going to be fine."

"I'm happy to hear you say that."

"Can I take you some place—to talk?"

"Where and when?" Raquel asked.

Keanu told her. She agreed.

"See you soon," he said eagerly and hung up, satisfied that things were back on track in their relationship.

He finished off the malt liquor while strategizing. There were a few things he needed to do between now and the first of the year. If everything worked out as he hoped, at that time Raquel would be well on her way to becoming Mrs. Keanu Bailey.

They drove down Kamehameha Highway toward the North Shore of Oahu. Less than an hour from Waikiki, it was one of Raquel's favorite places to hang out. She loved the cafes, fashionable boutiques, beaches, parks and museums there. She wondered why it had taken Keanu and her so long to go there together.

Better late than never, she thought.

Raquel gazed at his handsome profile as he drove, mostly in silence. When they did speak, it was more about general topics than about their relationship. Raquel felt it was a good sign that they were together at Keanu's request and that he had taken her away from Honolulu. She still found it hard to believe that they had gone from being in a professional relationship to a romantic relationship seemingly in no time at all. And now they could well be on the brink of becoming husband and wife, if Keanu still wanted this and had no doubts that she was the one for him.

He eyed her. "I thought you might like to know that I plan to officially launch my foundation on January first."

Raquel met his gaze. "That's wonderful."

Keanu grinned slightly. "It seemed like a nice way to start off the new year."

"I couldn't agree more. It must have kept you pretty busy."

He shrugged. "My lawyer and financial adviser have done much of the work. All I've had to do was sign some papers, make a few phone calls and take steps to set up a press conference. I hope it gets off to a strong start with finding partners to raise money for worthy causes."

"I can tell you've clearly thought this through." She gave him a toothy smile.

"It was your idea," he said. "I just wanted to make it happen and do what I probably should have done a long time ago."

"The important thing is that you're doing it now," she replied.

"You're right."

Raquel looked at him again and then gazed out the window. "So where exactly are we headed?"

Keanu smiled surreptitiously. "Oh, just a little place I thought you might like."

She was more than a tad curious.

Before long they arrived in Haleiwa, a historic town on the North Shore and Oahu's hub for art galleries and surf shops. They went to the North Shore Market Place and inside the Pearl Gallery, which featured art from Hawaiian artists.

"I never knew you were into art," Raquel said in awe, in spite of having seen a few obviously expensive works of art scattered throughout his mansion.

Keanu smiled. "I'm into a lot of things. This happens to be one of them. A few of my friends are artists and got me interested in art—especially paintings, stone and metal art and sculptures."

"I love that kind of art, too," she told him. "And also glass, local wood crafts and matted prints."

"I know," he said. "Lauren clued me in on your artistic tastes."

Raquel chuckled. "She never mentioned that to me."

"Guess she wanted to wait and see what I had in mind."

"I'm glad you brought me here," Raquel said.

Keanu gave her a half smile. "Let's go check out the gallery."

He took her hand and led Raquel around, looking at exhibits and even meeting some local artists. She enjoyed bonding like this on a different level.

"Do you want kids?" Raquel decided to just throw it out there to see exactly where he stood. *He's alluded to such, but never came right out with it.*

Keanu looked at her, stopping near a display of glass

art. "Yeah, I'd like to have some kids," he answered coolly. "Two or three might be nice."

She drew in a sigh of relief, but tried not to let it show. "I feel the same way."

He grinned. "That's good to know."

"Boys? Girls?"

"Both," he told her.

"Good answer," she said. "I've always wanted a girl to dote over the way my mother doted over me. But having a boy would be nice, too."

"I agree."

"Think you'd make a good father?" Raquel asked, knowing instinctively what his answer would be.

"I'd make a great father," Keanu responded boldly. "Probably spoil them rotten."

She laughed. "I could see that."

He laughed, too. "You'd make a great mom."

"You think so?"

"I *know* so, just like your own mom was to you."

"And still is," Raquel added thoughtfully.

Keanu planted a soft kiss on Raquel's lips, and she closed her eyes, savoring the moment. It seemed like forever before their mouths parted.

"Want to go back to my place?" Keanu asked, his deep eyes bearing down on her lustfully.

Raquel touched her lips, feeling a surge of desire swell within her. "I'd love to."

Chapter 14

The chime of his cell phone snapped Keanu back to consciousness. He had been dreaming of Raquel and hated that it was interrupted by someone calling. Squinty-eyed, he glanced at the clock. It was 2:00 a.m.

He glanced at Raquel lying next to him—his dream come true—before scooting out of bed naked to pick up his iPhone. Keanu did a double take when the caller ID identified the person calling as his friend Cassandra Tucker. His eyes fell on Raquel, as though she could see Cassie's name, but she was still sound asleep. Rather than wake her, he grabbed his cashmere robe and slipped out into the hall.

"Well, look who's calling," Keanu said, his ire at being awakened somewhat dampened.

"Surprise!" Cassandra said in her high-pitched voice.

"How long has it been?" He tried to recall when they

last spoke, and remembered that they last saw each other about six months ago. It was just after her divorce had become official and she had needed a shoulder to cry on. That hadn't lasted long, as she quickly moved on to a romance with a big-time Hollywood director.

"Probably like forever," she suggested.

"Yeah, I think so. Where the hell are you?"

"In New York. Why?"

"Because it's two in the morning here." Keanu gave a little nonchalant chuckle.

"Oh, I'm sorry for waking you up." Cassandra paused. "You were sleeping? Or did I disturb something else?"

"Only my beauty rest," he said.

"Oh, good. Guess I lost track of time given the different time zones."

"It's cool," Keanu said, knowing that absentmindedness was part of her character.

"So how have you been now that you're no longer running up and down the basketball court?" she asked.

He doubted she called at this hour to check on him, but humored her. "I'm good. Can't say I miss the heavy-duty team workouts or the constant travel."

"I know what you mean," Cassandra hummed. "Retirement at a young age sounds like much more fun."

Keanu thought about Raquel in bed and how much fun they'd been having between the sheets. And away from the bedroom. He definitely didn't want to see Cassandra mess that up in any way.

"Definitely," he said contemplatively. "So what's up?" He could hear her poodle yapping in the background.

"I've been working my ass off between my television series and two movies coming out next year," she whined. "I need to get away for a couple of days, to a private place where I won't be hounded by the paparazzi."

"You want to come out here—?" Keanu switched the phone to his other ear as if that would make any difference in his deduction.

"Yes!" Cassandra blurted out. "I know it's out of the blue, but your estate would be the perfect getaway for me to clear my head and get ready for next year's full schedule."

"I really feel for you, Cassie, and I'd be happy to help you out but—"

"Pleeeeease, Keanu," she broke in theatrically. "I wouldn't ask if it wasn't *really* important to me. I promise I'll stay out of your hair. Maybe take a dip in that fabulous pool of yours and work on my tan. Other than that, you'll never even know I'm there."

Normally Keanu would have gladly bent over backward to help out an old friend, especially one who had been there for him. But at a time when he was trying to show Raquel that she was the only woman for him and that he intended to make her his wife, allowing a beautiful ex-lover to stay with him, even for a couple of days, could cause more friction than he needed.

He sucked in a deep breath. "I understand your situation, Cassie. Thing is, I'm involved with someone right now and it might be kind of awkward if you came here and—"

"Say no more," Cassandra cut him off brusquely. "I shouldn't have called."

"I'm glad you did," Keanu fumbled with words. "It's always good to hear from you...."

He stopped when he heard the dial tone. She had hung up on him.

Raquel could make out the sounds of Keanu talking to someone, apparently on the phone. She yawned and looked at the clock. It was just after 2:00 a.m. Who was he talking to at this hour? Was it any of her business?

We just made love for hours and rededicated our love to each other in the process. He's obviously not involved with another woman. Or at least, he better not be.

She was trying not to get paranoid at this stage, regardless of his past and celebrity status.

Hearing the bedroom door open, Raquel tried to decide whether to pretend to be sleeping or not. She chose the latter.

"Hey," she said softly, making out Keanu's silhouette against the backdrop of a sheath of light filtering in from the hall.

"Hey," he said tonelessly.

"Were you talking on the phone?"

"Yeah. A friend called."

Raquel didn't want any secrets between them, even if she trusted Keanu. Besides, she wanted to get to know his friends. Or at least those who felt free to call at any hour of the day or night.

She waited for him to come back to bed. "Can I ask who?"

Keanu sighed, facing her. "Cassandra Tucker."

Raquel propped up on an elbow, more than a little curious. "And why was she calling?" As if she could forget his history of hobnobbing and more with one of Hollywood's leading ladies.

He pinched his nose. "Cassandra asked if she could get away from the business of Hollywood for a couple of days by staying at my place."

Raquel arched a brow. "Your place meaning here?"

"Yeah," Keanu said, eyes lowered.

"I can't believe this. She's got some nerve. I hope you told her no."

"Of course." He shrugged. "Didn't want you to get bent out of shape by having Cassie hanging around."

"What about *your* getting bent out of shape by having an ex-lover staying here when you're in a relationship now?" Raquel questioned.

Keanu took a breath. "To me it's no big deal. Before Cassie and I hooked up we were friends. Afterward we remained friends. Or am I not allowed to have female friends anymore?"

"I never said that. Excuse me for feeling a little insecure when your gorgeous former actress girlfriend comes calling. Does she even know you're with someone else now?" It occurred to Raquel that there was no reason for Cassandra to know unless he had maintained regular contact with her. Had he? Either way, it didn't sit well with her.

"She does now," Keanu said. "And there's no reason for you to feel insecure. First of all, you're gorgeous too and don't have to take a backseat to anyone in or out of Hollywood."

"And that's supposed to make me feel better?" Raquel asked. She heard the shrillness of her own voice and flushed.

"I don't know what you're getting so worked up

about, baby. I'm with you and not Cassandra Tucker, okay? You have absolutely nothing to worry about where it concerns her or any other woman. I told her she would have to find someplace else to stay for some R & R. She accepted that. End of story."

Raquel took a deep breath and closed her eyes to let his words sink in. She suddenly felt foolish, as though she were in a movie, playing the part of the needy, envious girlfriend. *Maybe I overreacted. If I can't trust Keanu to remain faithful to me, then why am I in this relationship with him?*

He had proven himself to be a changed man in a number of ways since she started working and sleeping with him. Would she be tempting fate if putting his loyalty to a test? Or by playing the jealous girlfriend, actually cause him to pull away or feel he was being smothered?

"I think you should invite Cassandra to come," Raquel said, surprising herself. She wasn't particularly keen on Cassandra making herself right at home in Keanu's mansion. But it seemed petty and insecure to want him all to herself to the exclusion of people he knew before her. After all, she had always loved everything Cassandra Tucker had appeared in and should be welcoming the opportunity to meet a first-rate actress in person. She might even pick up some interesting tidbits about Keanu from someone who may have had such knowledge.

"Where did this come from?" Keanu studied her wide-eyed.

"From a girlfriend who's had a sudden change of heart."

He sat on the bed. "I don't want a situation that makes you uncomfortable or—"

"If you truly believe that Cassandra is not out to try and win you back and you're comfortable letting her spend a couple of days here, I'm not going to insist she stays away from the island. Doesn't mean I won't be watching her."

Keanu grinned uneasily. "Wouldn't have it any other way. But as I said, you're the only woman in my life, so…"

"Then it's settled," Raquel said before she had a chance to change her mind. "Get back on the phone and tell Ms. Tucker that you and your *girlfriend* would love to have her drop in for a quick visit and getaway."

He chuckled. "*Mahalo.* You really are quite special, you know that?"

"Yes, but feel free to keep telling me as often as you like," she said, half joking.

Keanu kissed her on the lips, and Raquel savored the softness of his mouth. He got back up and dialed his phone, but this time he stayed in the room.

Hope I know what I'm getting myself into. Raquel sat up. Cassandra better be coming purely as a friend of Keanu's and nothing more. Even without knowing precisely what the future held, Raquel wasn't about to give up her man without a fight to the bitter end, even if she had to duke it out with Hollywood royalty.

As it was, Raquel suspected that Cassandra's romance calendar was probably full. Between what Keanu had told her and what she had read about Cassandra Tucker, men were literally tripping over themselves to get into her bed. And apparently more than a few had succeeded.

By the contented sound of Keanu's voice during his phone chat, it was obvious to Raquel that Cassandra Tucker had accepted his offer to put her up.

Keanu was admittedly a tad nervous when the limousine drove onto his property. It wasn't the first visit for Cassandra, who had shown up with an entourage for his birthday party a couple of years ago. But it was the first visit for a lady friend of his since he began dating Raquel. Though both women had more or less assured him that there would be no fireworks, Keanu still took a wait-and-see approach. For his part, he merely wanted to accommodate Cassie's request for a respite from the press and public.

But if he was being honest with himself, Keanu also wanted to show off his beautiful girlfriend to his ex and solicit advice from Cassandra on his designs to marry Raquel. If the two women could actually become friends in the process, he would consider that a bonus.

When the limousine pulled up to the house, Keanu was waiting alongside Raquel, who seemed genuinely excited at the prospect of meeting an A-list actress who had been dubbed the next Halle Berry. Also on hand to greet her were his uncle and Ashley, both of whom were fans of Cassandra.

As the limo driver opened the back door, Keanu held his breath. *Let the fun begin.*

Raquel's heart skipped a beat as she watched Cassandra Tucker emerge from the limousine as though about to step on the red carpet at the Academy Awards. She was holding an apricot-colored miniature poodle.

"Aloha, everyone," she said in a cheery voice.

"Aloha," came the response in chorus.

Keanu gave Cassandra a friendly hug. She returned this with air kisses to both cheeks.

"Pehea 'oe?" She asked how he was.

"Maika'i no au," Keanu said, telling her he was fine. "Good to see you again, Cassie."

"Better to see you, Keanu," she said. "You haven't changed a bit."

"I could say the same thing about you."

Her false lashes fluttered. "I'll take that as a compliment." She kissed the poodle. "You remember Boo Boo, don't you?"

Keanu smiled. "Yeah. Hey, Boo Boo." He ran a hand across the dog's fluffy coat, then turned to Raquel.

"You must be Raquel," Cassandra said before Keanu could introduce them.

Just how much has Keanu told you about me? Raquel tried to keep from shaking. "Yes."

"I'm Cassandra, but please call me Cassie." Her teeth glimmered as though just polished.

"All right." Raquel smiled. "Nice to meet you, Cassie."

"You, too."

Raquel sized her up. Taller and thinner than she seemed on the screen, she was every bit as gorgeous in person. Cassandra had high cheekbones, small nighttime eyes and a cappuccino complexion. Her long ink-black hair was slick with blunt angles and thick bangs. Raquel wondered if she'd had collagen put into those pouty lips. As though en route to a Hollywood premiere, rather than a Hawaiian retreat, Cassandra wore a low-cut, formfitting, beryl blue satin dress and high-heeled espadrilles.

Raquel noted that Cassandra was checking her out, too. Knowing she couldn't possibly compete with Cassandra in terms of expensive designer attire, she chose instead to keep her own clothing simple yet stylish. She wore a white tab sleeve shirt with a gray pencil skirt and wedge sandals.

Keanu introduced Cassandra to Ashley and reacquainted her with his Uncle Sonny. In spite of what was only supposed to be a two-day trip, Raquel noted that the limo driver had laid out enough baggage on the ground to cover a month's stay.

Even if this made a small part of her ill at ease, Raquel was more amused than anything by the typical excesses of Hollywood stars. She could only wonder how this weekend would play out.

Keanu showed Cassandra to her suite, leaving her to unpack some of her things. She still looked great and, no doubt, had broken another heart in her merry-go-round of failed relationships. He hoped the rest and relaxation did what she hoped so he could get back to his own life, minus her drama.

He found Raquel downstairs chatting with Ashley. Seemed like a good thing to him if she and his uncle's wife could bond. Might be a nice stepping stone toward the family Keanu hoped to find with Raquel, just as his uncle had with Ashley.

Raquel looked up when Keanu walked into the living room. "Ashley was just telling me that she used to be a hula dancer," she said animatedly.

"Is that right?"

"It was a long time ago," Ashley said. "My girlfriend

roped me into it on a dare. It was fun for a while, but grew old quickly."

He tried to picture her as a younger woman dancing at a luau. "Maybe you could teach Raquel a thing or two," he joked.

"I think it might be more the opposite," she countered. "The modern-day dancers have a lot more moves and flexibility than I ever had."

"I'm still a work in progress," Raquel said with a chuckle.

Keanu regarded her approvingly. "And progressing very nicely, I might add."

She batted her lashes demurely. "You would say that."

"Listen to the man," Ashley chimed in. "Keanu clearly knows what he wants—and who."

Keanu's eyes glinted, appreciating her support. He tucked his arms around Raquel's waist. "Absolutely," he said, planting a kiss on her lips.

They stepped out on a lanai and resumed the kiss.

Raquel took her lips from beneath his. "Keep that up and you'll get exactly what you want, time and time again."

Keanu wiped his mouth. "I'm counting on that," he said with desire.

"So where's your guest anyway?"

"In her room," he said. "She should be joining us shortly."

"Sure she brought enough clothes?" Raquel asked.

Keanu chuckled. "Be nice."

"I'll try," she promised.

"I think you two could become friends."

She rolled her eyes. "The over-the-top Hollywood

actress and the down-to-earth image consultant from Honolulu? Not so sure about that."

He kissed her again. "Sounds like a perfect match to me. Also, she knows a lot of people more screwed up than I ever was. Play your cards right, and Cassie could send you more business than you know what to do with."

Raquel raised a brow. "Hmm...that's certainly something to ponder."

Keanu smiled. "Thought it might be." He kissed her again, and this time their lips remained locked in perpetual motion. All Keanu could think about was wishing they were in the privacy of his bedroom right now.

The passion was broken when Keanu heard a sound. He turned and saw Cassandra.

"Hey," she said awkwardly, holding her poodle. "Hope I'm not interrupting—"

You are, but I'll deal with it. "Not at all." He grinned and made it seem genuine.

Cassandra had changed into something more comfortable and appropriate: a sleeveless knit top, cuffed jean shorts and flats, making Raquel feel almost overdressed. But then again, she hadn't come with more than a few outfits to mix and match. And unless she and Keanu were actually living together, Raquel had no plans to keep extra clothes at his house, aside from her swimsuit.

Keanu had gone to buy a Christmas tree with Sonny and Ashley, leaving her to keep Cassandra company. Raquel wouldn't be too surprised if Keanu had planned it to see if they could get along without any negative energy.

That was fine by Raquel, as she welcomed some time alone with someone she admired as an accomplished actress, if not a role model for stability and faithfulness in a relationship. She could only imagine what Lauren would say had she known Cassandra Tucker was in town and staying at Keanu's estate. They sat at a poolside table and sipped tropical drinks while Boo Boo lay quietly nearby.

"I have to say that I never miss an episode of your show *Dark Intentions*," Raquel said.

"That's nice to hear." Cassandra flushed. "I can tell you that the series has just been renewed for a fourth season."

"Congratulations."

"Thanks," Cassandra said. "It's a fun show to do when I'm not making movies."

Raquel wasn't sure if she was showing off or being sincere. "You've had a great career."

"Yes, but with that comes expectations and pressures," Cassandra complained over her drink. "Being in Hollywood is not always everything it's cracked up to be."

"I suppose that's true with most things," Raquel said and tossed a cashew in her mouth.

"Sometimes it's good to get away from it all."

Raquel met her eyes. "Like now?"

Cassandra gave her a weak smile. "Yes, exactly."

"I think I can relate to some degree," Raquel said.

Cassandra sipped her drink. "Living in paradise as you do, it's hard to imagine anyone ever wanting to leave."

"Yes, it is paradise," agreed Raquel. "But it's also like any other place that has its ups and downs."

Cassandra nodded thoughtfully. "Makes sense." She spoke to her dog and got a bark in response. "So I understand Keanu hired you to work on his image?"

"He did."

"I know a few people who could probably benefit from your talents," Cassandra said.

"Feel free to give them my number." She took a card out of her bag and handed it to Cassandra.

"I'll do that," she promised and gazed at her deliberately. "According to Keanu, he got so much more in return than reshaping his image from his association with you."

"I think we've both gotten a lot more," Raquel said candidly, glancing at the ocean and back.

"So I hear." Cassandra scratched her dainty nose. "It's plain to see that you two are really into each other."

"Yes, we are," Raquel said happily.

"Keanu's a great guy...."

"I agree." Raquel paused. "I know you and he were—"

"We hooked up a while back," Cassandra admitted easily. "It was an instant connection and we were both at a certain place and time in our lives. It was never serious."

"You don't have to explain that to me," Raquel said. She didn't need to know the details of her boyfriend's tryst with a Hollywood star.

"I know that, but I wanted to. I'm sure it must feel awkward having me here, under the circumstances. Just wanted to clear the air. I'm only in town as a friend with no designs on going after your man."

"I appreciate your saying that." Raquel felt some

sense of relief. "Keanu's asked me to marry him, if he hadn't already mentioned it to you."

Cassandra arched a thin brow in clear shock. "Oh, really? I didn't realize Keanu had finally found *true* love. And in the perfect setting. Congratulations—"

Raquel was a little surprised that Keanu hadn't mentioned this to her. Why not? Was he hoping to keep it to himself while his ex-girlfriend was visiting? Perhaps a reflection of the playboy in him that hadn't quite disappeared altogether?

"I didn't say yes, yet," Raquel told her.

"Really?" Cassandra looked at her. "Getting cold feet?"

"Not exactly." She explained her delay in agreeing to marry Keanu.

"Actually, that was probably a good move on your part," Cassandra said, leaning forward and tasting her drink.

"You think?" Raquel batted her lashes.

"Yes. Give him something to think about so he doesn't take you for granted. It also allows you time to make sure you're ready to marry an athlete, even if he is a real hottie who obviously adores you."

Raquel met her gaze. "Sounds like you've been down this road before." She vaguely recalled reading once that Cassandra had dated a professional athlete.

"I have," she said. "I was engaged to a football player named Otis Foxworth. I was just getting started in the acting business and fell hard for Otis and all those muscles. We seemed like a match made in heaven. But you know what? We weren't. With Otis's constant travel, not to mention my own, and rumors flying left and right about both of us…well, it all just got to be too much.

We both realized our love for each other was not strong enough so we decided to go our separate ways. I sometimes wonder if I made a mistake. But since Otis and I have had trouble to this day holding on to relationships, I'd say we made the right decision."

"Interesting," was all Raquel could say, realizing Cassandra had described some of her own concerns about marrying Keanu. Would the bad habits from his days as an athlete resurface like a bad dream down the road, putting strain on their relationship?

"Don't get me wrong," Cassandra said, as though reading her mind. "I'm not suggesting you walk away from Keanu, far from it. He'd kill me if I said that."

Raquel chuckled humorlessly. "But you are speaking as the voice of experience...."

"Your situation is somewhat different from mine," she pointed out. "Keanu is retired now and no longer into the lifestyle of professional athletes that can get them into trouble. It looks like he's settled into his hometown and found someone special to share his life with."

"But is that enough?" Raquel asked straightforwardly. "How can I be sure?"

"Trust your instincts," Cassandra said. "If you believe that you and Keanu have what it takes to make a lasting marriage, then don't let my experience or anyone else's two cents detract from that."

My instincts are usually spot-on. Raquel's eyes crinkled as she contemplated the words of wisdom from someone who obviously understood exactly what her own anxieties were. "*Mahalo,* Cassie."

"No problem at all." Cassandra lifted her drink. "I

wish you and Keanu the best, whatever direction you decide to go in."

The best was all Raquel wanted from their relationship and their future. She believed Keanu wanted this too. With the year winding down, she wondered if he would ask her to marry him again. Or was that something he preferred to put on hold indefinitely while he clung to bachelorhood and an independent lifestyle?

For now, she just wanted to enjoy being with a man who had changed his life for the better and allowed Raquel to discover the love she had always found so elusive.

Chapter 15

After they had found the perfect Christmas tree, Keanu, Sonny and Ashley brought it home. With his guests on hand, they decorated it, then put up some outside lights and a door wreath, thereby readying the estate for the holiday season.

Keanu was happy to see that Raquel and Cassandra seemed to get along well in his absence, which had been one reason he left the two women alone. He needed to know that Raquel could handle him having female friends and still want to be his girlfriend. By all accounts, she had passed the test. Moreover, it appeared as though she and Cassie genuinely liked each other. That meant Cassandra just might make the return trip to paradise when he and Raquel walked down the aisle. Keanu savored the thought of making Raquel his bride and giving her the type of life he could provide and she deserved.

In bed that night, Raquel was all over Keanu like a woman possessed. She kissed his face, chest, the tattoos on his arms and then went back to Keanu's lips. She sucked on his lower lip, stuck her tongue in his mouth and rode him hard as her body straddled him. His own libido heightened by the aggressive woman on top of him, Keanu gripped her sides, lifting Raquel up and down on his erection. She moaned with each thrust, her luscious hair falling on his face while they kissed torridly.

Her constrictions grew stronger as the intensity of their lovemaking brought both to the brink of an orgasm. He turned them over so he was on top and put his face between Raquel's breasts, licking the silken valley before sucking on her nipples. She cried salaciously, trembling wildly while slamming into him. Keanu's heart raced and his body dripped with perspiration as their moment came to enjoy the height of mutual pleasure.

Each held the other tightly and let the impact of sexual gratification absorb through their paralyzed bodies and senses. At the end of the journey, Keanu rolled off his lover, content with what may have been their best lovemaking yet.

"You never fail to amaze me," he said, sighing against her cheek.

"I could say the same thing about you," she said.

"Just keeps getting better all the time."

"So it seems," she agreed. "Must be the company we're keeping."

Keanu chuckled softly. "Yeah, that has to be it." He

kissed her chin and lips. "Definitely damned good company I keep with you."

"Ditto," Raquel told him. "Hope we didn't disturb your other houseguest."

He grinned. "These walls are soundproof. My guess is that Cassie and Boo Boo sleep like babies, when they're not awake and wailing."

"I'm glad Cassie came," she said, adjusting in his arms. "I really like her. She's pretty cool and not at all difficult like the media portrays her to be."

"I agree," he told her. "I'm glad you two got to hang out."

"Speaking of…why didn't you tell her you asked me to marry you?"

"There was nothing really to tell seeing that you never gave me a definitive answer."

"I know," Raquel conceded. "I just thought you'd want to let her know how seriously involved you were with another woman."

"I think she knows that," Keanu said. "It's obvious to anyone who can see that I'm crazy about you."

"Hmm…so was that your secret plan in inviting Cassie? To show off your lady?"

Keanu held Raquel a bit more snugly. "Maybe I did want her to see what a catch I had in you. But I also wanted you to see that I'm totally over her and that she and I are just friends."

"I believe you," said Raquel. "Sorry if I came across as the jealous girlfriend."

"It's cool. I understand that with my background, there might be some lingering doubts." He kissed her hair. "I'm prepared to show you that I really have changed for the better. And it's all because of you."

"It had better be," she said playfully. "I take my job very seriously. And my man even more so."

Keanu smiled. "Glad to know that, since I feel the same way."

He kissed the side of her face till Raquel turned and gave him her lips.

The following morning, Keanu watched as Raquel rolled out of bed to get dressed.

"Sure you don't want to go another round?" he asked, staring at her appealing body.

"Tempting, but I have to go to work." She slipped into her underwear. "Besides, I don't want to monopolize all of your time while Cassie's here."

"She'll understand."

"No reason for her to," Raquel said. "She's your friend who came to spend a few days at your house. The least you can do is entertain her and that cute poodle, without your girlfriend hanging around as if she has to watch your every move."

"True, but—"

"No buts," she told him firmly. "Have fun with her. Who knows, maybe one day we can go check out one of her movie premieres."

"Sounds like fun," Keanu said, sure that Cassandra would be happy to oblige.

That afternoon, he took a walk on the beach with Cassandra, who had Boo Boo on a leash.

"It's so nice and peaceful here," Cassandra said enviously.

"Helps when you have your own secluded stretch of beach," Keanu told her with a grin.

"Yes, it does." She smiled and gazed out at the

ocean. "Maybe I'll invest in some property in Honolulu."

"Not a bad idea," he said, though doubtful she would ever follow through. The Cassandra Tucker he knew was too much into the fast life of New York City and Los Angeles to find happiness in the more laid-back lifestyle of Hawaii.

"Do you think we could have made a go of it, had the circumstances been different?" she asked.

Keanu's brows lifted, not expecting the question. "Probably not," he responded honestly. "Let's face it, with our fast-paced lives at the time we would never have gotten very far."

"I think you're probably right." Cassandra turned to him. "I'd say you've found the right woman to build a future with."

"You really think so?" Keanu asked.

"Absolutely. Raquel's stunning, smart, successful in her own right and thinks the world of you. What's not to be highly impressed with?"

His cheeks rose. "Nothing that I can see."

"Oh, and did I forget to add that she's obviously done her job by helping your image," Cassandra said. "I've been keeping tabs on you."

Keanu raised a brow. "Have you now?"

She smiled, nodding. "I know you're trying to do the right thing now that you're retired and holed up in this heaven on earth."

"I have," he acknowledged.

"And Raquel has a lot to do with that. Am I right?"

"You are." Keanu was more than happy to admit what a ray of light Raquel had been in his life on multiple fronts.

"So when are you going to ask her to marry you again?" Cassandra asked. "And please don't tell me you're thinking about taking back your proposal."

Keanu chuckled. "I haven't decided yet," he said. "I don't want to put any pressure on her or myself. I just hope if and when such a time comes that she'll say yes. A man can only wait so long for a woman to think about it."

"Women always need time to think about it," she told him. "It's when we don't that we run into trouble, and you end up paying for it one way or the other. Trust me when I tell you that Raquel loves you to death and wants to be your wife. I think she just wants to be certain *you* are ready to be her husband, so *she* isn't left holding the bag."

"I get it," he muttered.

"Do you?"

He met her eyes, having thought about this long enough. "Yeah, I know it's on me. I haven't had the best reputation when it comes to romance, which I'm sure you can relate to."

"I'm sure I can," she told him dryly.

"But with Raquel, I feel things I never have for a woman before. She's the real deal for me."

"Then tell her as many times as necessary. And let her know she has nothing to worry about and that you're going into this without any uncertainty whatsoever."

"Good advice," Keanu said thoughtfully.

"If and when you're ready to take the plunge, don't forget the engagement ring," Cassandra said, smiling. "Us women like them big and expensive. Make it something to remember, and Raquel's heart will melt."

A grin spread across his face. "Spoken like a woman who's been there."

"More than once," she noted, laughing. "But who's counting? Each time is just as special as the last."

"I'm sure," Keanu said.

Cassandra glanced at her dog rolling around in the sand and then fixed her eyes on Keanu's face. "*Dark Intentions* will be on hiatus next summer. The wedding of one of my dearest friends would be a good excuse to return to Hawaii next year. Hint, hint."

Keanu laughed. "I'll keep that in mind. But we wouldn't want to get ahead of ourselves here. Let's just wait and see if things go that way or not. Right now I think I'll just take it one day at a time and enjoy what Raquel and I have."

"You met Cassandra Tucker in the flesh and didn't tell me she was in town?" Lauren gave Raquel a scathing look.

"I wanted to," Raquel said apologetically as they stood in her living room putting up Christmas decorations. "But she wanted to keep her visit under wraps so the press didn't get wind of it."

"But I'm your *best* friend—or at least I thought I was," Lauren pouted. "And I happen to be a *big* fan of Cassandra's."

"I know," Raquel said guiltily. "I did get her to autograph a magazine I had with her on the cover—for you."

Lauren's face brightened. "How thoughtful."

"Better yet, given her friendship with Keanu, I wouldn't be surprised at all if Cassie showed up here again sometime.…"

Lauren hoisted a brow. "Cassie now, is it? I am so jealous."

"Don't be," Raquel told her. "She's just like you and me when you get right down to it. She just happens to be an actress." And someone who Keanu once had the hots for. But Raquel was sure that was ancient history.

"Yeah, right." Lauren rolled her eyes. "Easy for you to say now that you've become best buds with the hottest actress around right now."

Okay, I'd better change the subject. "If Keanu and I ever get married, it's you who will be my maid of honor," Raquel assured her.

Lauren eyed her. "Don't you mean when?"

"I'd rather not put the cart ahead of the horse. Keanu has not proposed again. But we've been spending a lot of time together lately and things between us seem better than ever, so—"

"So you figure it's only a matter of time?"

"Maybe so and maybe no," Raquel said. "If it's meant to happen it will, if not…"

The fact that Keanu hadn't asked her to marry him again indicated that he was at least taking his own sweet time. Which was the point, wasn't it? She didn't want it to be a rash decision they could both wind up regretting.

Now that the dust had settled a bit and they had picked up their smoking romance, Raquel counted her blessings that she and Keanu were a couple, whether married or not. As for another proposal, the ball was now in Keanu's court.

"I'm not there quite yet with Victor either," Lauren said. "We're also letting things work themselves out in our relationship. But we're both definitely pulling for you and Keanu to make it all official."

Raquel smiled. "I'm hopeful that everything will work out for you too, girlfriend. In the meantime, we'd better get back to decorating. Christmas will be here before you know it."

On Christmas Day, Keanu, Sonny and Ashley welcomed Davetta, Sean and Raquel to their home.

"Mele Kalikimaka," Keanu told all, meaning Merry Christmas. He gave Davetta a hug and kissed her cheek.

"Mele Kalikimaka," she said. *"Mahalo* for inviting us."

"It's our pleasure to have you," Sonny told her, grinning. "We already feel as if Raquel is part of the family."

"That's nice to hear," her mother said, beaming at Raquel.

"I do feel right at home here these days," she admitted.

Keanu planted a soulful kiss on Raquel's ruby lips to let her know that she was his family, for all intents and purposes. He could envision them living in that house—or another home together one day.

"Why don't we give you the grand tour now," Ashley said.

"I can already tell you've got quite a place here," Sean marveled, looking up at the architectural splendor.

Sonny patted him on the shoulder. "It's our little slice of heaven."

Keanu felt good knowing that his uncle had fully embraced the estate as theirs to share. It was certainly large enough for everyone to have their own space, with room to spare. Moreover, he was encouraged that Sonny and Sean seemed headed toward friendship. As Sean seemed like a fixture in Davetta's life, Keanu wanted to treat him like family too, which would show Raquel that he considered this a package deal.

Keanu and Raquel stayed in the living room while the house was being shown. Donny Hathaway's romantic tune "This Christmas" permeated through the air, as the entire place was wired for sound. Keanu held Raquel's hand as they walked up to the Christmas tree to look at its colored lights and decorations.

"I'm delighted we get to spend our first Christmas together," he told her.

"So am I," she said.

"I like having someone to play Santa Claus for."

Raquel licked her lips. "Oh, do you now?"

"Yeah," Keanu said, leaning in to taste those full lips of hers.

"And what does Santa have for me this year?" she asked.

"Well, now, that all depends on whether or not you've been a good little girl," he said mischievously.

Her eyes twinkled. "I'm always good, except when you prefer the bad girl to come out."

Keanu tossed his head back with a laugh, feeling aroused at how bad she could be in bed. "In that case, I do have a little something for you that I thought I'd give you before the formal unwrapping of gifts."

"Please don't keep me in suspense any longer," Raquel said.

He smiled at her. "All right, I won't."

From the look in her eyes, Keanu suspected that she might be expecting an engagement ring. He hoped she wasn't too disappointed in the Christmas gift he'd chosen to get her.

Keanu bent down and grabbed a small box from beneath the tree. It wasn't wrapped. Standing up again, he presented the box to her. "Hope you like…"

She wasted no time in removing the box top. Inside was a princess cut, nine-carat diamond bracelet.

"It's beautiful," gushed Raquel.

"You're beautiful," Keanu said. He removed the bracelet and put it around her slender wrist. "It looks great against your honey-brown skin."

She flexed her arm. "Yes, it does. But this bracelet must have cost you a small fortune."

"No amount of money is too much for someone you love," he said.

Their eyes met. "That doesn't mean you have to buy me such expensive gifts."

"If not for you, then who?" His brows lowered. "I have plenty of money, Raquel, and up till now, no one that I really wanted to spend it on. So indulge me and just enjoy it as much as I enjoy your being in my life."

She batted her eyes. "Well, when you put it that way, how can I not be happy with this diamond bracelet, just as I am with the man who gave it to me?"

"Exactly," he said, bearing a grin.

Raquel ran her hand along his cheek. "You are so good to me. What did I ever do to deserve you?"

"Just by being who you are and giving me a reason to smile each and every day."

She lifted her chin and brought their mouths together, both savoring the long, soft kiss.

Keanu felt a tickle as Raquel's warm breath fell on

his cheek. He pulled back, staring into her eyes, and said what seemed so apropos on this special day, "*Mele Kalikimaka,* baby."

Chapter 16

On New Year's Eve, Raquel lined up with the other hula dancers at a Waikiki Beach resort hotel in a colorful costume, with a lei headpiece and necklace to put on a show for tourists and locals. It was everything she expected it to be, and more, and Keanu was in attendance. Her eyes sparkled at him as she shook her hips and her arms swayed in perpetual motion. All of the dancers followed the exotic choreographed moves to the sounds of Hawaiian, Fijian and Tongan music.

Raquel's mind wandered to the last four-plus months and the romance that had consumed her. Keanu had started off as a client with an image problem and had become the man of her dreams, whom she couldn't imagine a life without. She glanced at the diamond bracelet on her wrist. Though it had not been the engagement ring Raquel had thought Keanu might give her for Christmas, it was just as cherished—a true symbol of his love for her. Since she had held off accepting his proposal the first time, she was content to wait it out for as long as he wanted. She had made it clear how much she loved him and he, in turn, had illustrated the power of his affection through the bracelet. It was evident that he had put his bad boy ways behind him.

But Keanu had remained as popular as ever in Hawaii, and Raquel fully supported this, seeing no reason why he shouldn't bask in his success and the brand he'd created. The new and improved Keanu Bailey was even more in demand as a retired and marketable athlete. She thought back to the Honolulu City Lights, a Christmastime event with free concerts and a parade that wound its way through downtown and Chinatown. Keanu had graciously participated, much to the delight of his fans and girlfriend.

Raquel's teeth gleamed as she came back to the present and waved at Keanu while keeping pace with the other dancers, including her friend Kym. She loved the music and the show, but even more she loved having a man in her life who supported her dancing and career.

Keanu was smitten as ever while he watched Raquel perform. It was undoubtedly something she was born to do, just as he was born to play basketball. He was even more excited about the beginning of the new year that would mark a turning point in their relationship.

"You were fabulous, baby," he told Raquel after her stirring performance. He gave her a long kiss.

"Of course," she said, grinning. "How could I not be with my man watching every move?"

Keanu laughed. "You've got that right."

Raquel flipped her hair back. "It's just about midnight."

"Yeah," he noted, grabbing two glasses with champagne and handing her one. "Here's to the New Year and making the most of it."

"I'll definitely drink to that," she said gleefully, raising her glass to his.

The countdown had begun. Ten, nine, eight, seven, six, five, four, three, two, one…

"Hau'oli Makahiki Hou!" Keanu and Raquel joined the chorus of others saying Happy New Year in Hawaiian.

Keanu leaned Raquel over and gave her a lip-smacking kiss.

"Wow!" Raquel tasted her mouth. "What a sweet way to break into the New Year!"

"I'll second that," Keanu said, and kissed her again.

Raquel smiled joyously. "More of that later. Right now you've got a press conference to give."

He nodded coolly. "Let's get out of here."

Keanu talked casually during the drive to his house. He had invited a network camera crew, along with friends and his financial adviser for the 1:00 a.m. press announcement followed by a question-and-answer session. He didn't want to tip his hand that the foundation was only part of what he wanted to talk about.

"Maybe during the spring we can vacation somewhere on the mainland," he suggested.

"Anywhere you want to go is fine by me," Raquel said.

"Cool." He offered her a serious look. "I was thinking we could stop over in Detroit, introduce you to some of my old teammates, and finish off in New York or Boston."

"Sounds like a plan, honey."

"Great," he said, giving her a warm smile.

When they arrived at Keanu's house, his study was already set up and the crew had arrived, interested in hearing him provide details about his new foundation.

He greeted his financial adviser and friends, whom his Uncle Sonny and Ashley had been entertaining, before moving to the podium.

After assessing his audience, particularly Raquel, Keanu took a breath and collected his thoughts. "Thank you for coming as we start the New Year. I'll keep it brief so you can get back to your partying and such. I'd like to announce the formation of my new nonprofit venture, the Keanu L. Bailey Foundation. Its mission will be to fund research to fight cancer, diabetes, sickle cell anemia, heart disease and other illnesses. In addition to putting up the initial funding to jump-start the foundation, I will also be sponsoring fundraising events to get others to join me in fighting these and other medical conditions. I will also be headed to Africa this summer to participate in the Basketball Without Borders program. Should be a lot of fun."

Keanu was stopped due to applause. When it died down, he continued. "I owe my involvement in this nonprofit foundation and BWB to a very special lady in my life, Raquel Deneuve." He gazed at her as others cheered. "Can you come up here for a moment, Raquel?"

She gave him a surprised look and moved up next to him. "This is about *you,* not me," she whispered.

He gave her a big grin. "I beg to differ. It's very much about both of us, baby."

She fluttered her lashes uneasily. "Hmm…"

After staring into her curious eyes for a moment or two, Keanu was ready to make his move. He put his hand in the pocket of his lambswool sport coat and removed a small box. Opening it, he revealed an engagement ring with a 4.02-carat yellow diamond bordered by sparkling side stones in platinum and eighteen-karat gold.

He fell to one knee and placed the ring on her finger. It was a perfect fit. Gazing up at Raquel's shocked face, Keanu asked calmly, "Raquel Deneuve, will you marry me? Please say yes and make me the happiest man on the islands on New Year's Day."

Raquel put a trembling hand to her mouth and then studied the luminous ring. With a glow in her watering eyes, she gazed down at Keanu. "Yes, Keanu Bailey, I will marry you!"

There was an eruption of cheers and clapping. Keanu rose to his feet and stared at the face before him that had never looked more beautiful than at this moment. "Aloha *au ia 'oe,*" he said, tenderly declaring his love.

"Aloha *nui loa.*" Raquel said that she loved him very much, too.

Nearly overcome with emotion, Keanu did the one thing that could seal the deal. He held Raquel's face and pressed their mouths together in a kiss fit for a lifetime of bliss in paradise.

* * * * *

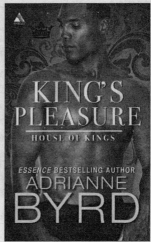

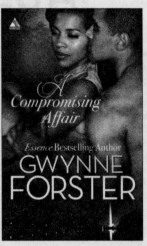

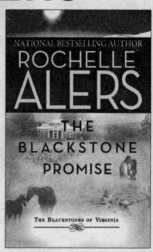

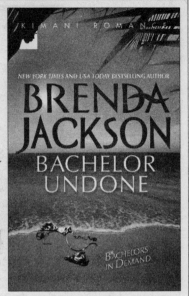